Upon A Winter's Night

A MacKinnon's Rangers Christmas Novella

By Pamela Clare

Upon A Winter's Night

A MacKinnon's Rangers Christmas Novella

By Pamela Clare

Published by Pamela Clare, 2013

Cover image by Jenn LeBlanc/Studio Smexy™
Cover design by Seductive Designs

Copyright © 2013 by Pamela Clare

ISBN-10: 0983875995
ISBN-13: 978-0-9838759-9-4

Dedication

This novella is dedicated to the members of the Facebook Camp Followers group. Thank you for sharing your love of history — and these characters — with me.

Acknowledgements

With thanks to Eileen Hannay and Gary Zaboly, whose passion for history both inspires and informs me.

Additional thanks to Michelle White; Benjamin Alexander; Joyce Lamb; Kristin Anders, The Romantic Editor; Stephanie Desprez; and Rachel Daven Skinner for the moral support, formatting, and copy editing.

CHAPTER ONE

December 18, 1760
North of Albany
His Majesty's Colony of New York

Connor MacKinnon strode toward the barn, snow squeaking beneath his moccasins, the icy air biting his nose, sunrise a glimmer of gold in the east. "*Madainn mhath*," he called to his brother Morgan, who was busy chopping firewood near the woodpile.

Good morning.

Ax in hand, Morgan glowered at him, kicked a piece of firewood into the pile. "What's so bloody good about it?"

Och, hell.

So that was the way of things.

Connor let his brother's words go. To his way of thinking, there was much about this day that was good and right. The war was over. The MacKinnon farm had been prosperous, yielding a bountiful harvest to see them through the cold and dark of winter. Most of all, he and his brothers had each taken a bonny lass to wife and had five strong bairns between them — four lads and a lass.

Aye, God had been good to them.

If someone had told him this time last year that he'd be happily wed to the niece of his greatest enemy, Connor would have thought them daft. But such was the way of it, and he could not have felt more blessed.

You're a lucky bastard, MacKinnon.

He entered the dark warmth of the barn. Cows lowed, eager to be milked, the air pungent with the scents of hay, leather, and manure. He passed the well-ordered and oiled horse tack and farm gear and walked to the back where Iain was already measuring out the morning's portion of oats for the horses.

Iain looked up. *"Madainn mhath."*

"Dia dhuit." God be with you.

Connor patted Frìthe, his favorite mare, on her velvety muzzle. "Morgan's in a rage again."

"Aye. So I noticed." Iain handed Connor a filled nosebag. "Annie says Amalie has forsaken his bed altogether."

Och, well, that would be enough to sour any man's temper.

Connor slipped the nosebag onto Frìthe's head, and the mare began to feed. "Yule is but a week hence. 'Tis no' fittin' that he and Amalie find themselves still at odds. Talk wi' him, Iain. You are the eldest. He'll heed your counsel."

Iain handed Connor another nosebag of oats. "I've tried talkin' wi' him, but he willna listen. 'Tis worry that drives him. I've no words to assuage such fears."

Nor did Connor.

These were not baseless fears, but fears born from harsh reality. Women perished in childbed every day, dying as they struggled to bring new life into the world. Only two weeks had passed since Sarah had given birth to little William, and Connor would never forget her long hours of suffering, the chilling sound of her cries, or the fear that had gnawed at him as he'd wondered whether she and the child would both survive.

And yet to hear Iain and Morgan speak of it, Sarah's travail had been blessedly brief and easy compared to that which Amalie had endured. Last March, Amalie had borne Morgan twin sons and would certainly have perished had Rebecca, a skilled midwife and sister to their Mahican blood brother Joseph Aupauteunk, not been here to help with the birth.

Aye, Connor could understand why Morgan had refused to lie with his wife in the customary way. Morgan did not wish to see her suffer again, nor did he wish to risk losing her. But nine months had now passed since the twins' birth, and Amalie's patience seemed to be at an end. If, as Iain's wife, Annie, had said, Amalie had forsaken Morgan's bed altogether, there would be no living with either of them.

Connor carried the nosebag to Fiona's stall, hung it gently on the mare's head. "Somethin' must be done. I dinnae wish to see Amalie weepin' at Christmas, and I've grown weary of Morgan's sharp tongue."

"As have I." Iain began to fill two more nosebags.

An idea came to Connor, which he kept to himself.

"How does Sarah fare?" Iain asked, breaking the momentary silence. "Last night couldna have been easy for her."

Last night, the English lord Connor had once vowed to kill had come back from the dead to pay them a visit. Lord William Wentworth, Sarah's uncle, had crept up to their door in the dark of night, leaving a letter from England and a single chess piece — a king made of cracked black marble — on the step of their cabin. Alerted to his presence by the hounds, Connor and his brothers had tried for Sarah's sake to find him and invite him in out of the cold. But the bastard had turned his horse's head toward Albany and ridden as if Satan himself were at his heels, refusing to see them or to be seen by them. Though relieved to know her uncle, who'd been taken captive last summer by the Wyandot Indians, was alive, Sarah had been heartbroken by his refusal to see her.

"She's keepin' the chess piece in her apron pocket. I've seen her take it out and close her hand around it. But she's no' spoken a word of her uncle today."

"And the letter?"

Connor did not truly wish to talk about that, but he knew Iain would push him harder if he didn't answer. "It lies atop her harpsichord."

Curse that letter!

Written to Wentworth, it revealed how Sarah's name had been cleared of any taint and said that the scandal that had caused her parents to send her to the Colonies had been resolved. Connor knew he should welcome that news with a full heart, but, despite Sarah's assurances that she loved him and wanted to remain with him, some part of him feared she would one day wish to leave the hardships and uncertainties of life on the frontier and return to London to reclaim her place in society.

Not that it would be easy for her to return should she wish it. All of Britain believed her dead, slain in the same battle in which Wentworth had been taken captive. But Sarah was descended from royalty. If she truly wished to return to England, her uncle would find a way to make it happen. What gently bred lady would truly wish to live in a frontier cabin working her hands to the bone when she could live in splendor with servants to tend her?

"She misses Wentworth." Iain handed Connor the feed bags.

"Aye, she does." Connor carried the feed bags to their two big draft horses, geldings named Dubh and Donaidh, patting them each on the neck.

"How strange it is that I find myself bound to a man whom I once would gladly have slain."

Through Connor and Sarah's union, noble MacKinnon blood mingled with that of the House of Hanover in newborn William's veins.

"Aye, 'tis hard to fathom." Iain chuckled. "If ever you see him again, I suppose you'll be callin' him *Uncle* William."

Connor glared at his brother. "Not bloody likely."

"Your son bears his name." A grin tugged at Iain's lips.

"*I* named him after William Wallace. 'Tis Sarah who thinks we've named him after Wentworth, and I willna dissuade her from believin' that if it pleases her."

Connor had just started up the ladder to the hayloft to pitch hay into the cow pen when a voice came from outside. "Hallo in the house!"

He and Iain broke into grins as they recognized Joseph's voice.

They strode out of the barn together in time to see Joseph, their Mahican blood brother, leap down from the seat of a small wagon, a shaggy gray horse in the harness. Wearing a thick bearskin robe to ward off the cold, a single eagle feather in his long dark hair, he nodded in greeting to them.

"Dinnae be tellin' me you've taken to travelin' by wagon," Iain teased. "Have you grown soft wi'out the war to keep you fit?"

Grinning, Joseph tied off the reins, his cheeks red from cold. "I am not the one who sits before a warm fire growing fat like an old bear."

"'Tis a shame you've no pretty wife to cook for you, but then I suppose no woman will have you," Iain mocked.

Connor walked forward, rubbed the horse's muzzle. "Your wagon has seen better days, brother, but this is a fine animal."

"This is not mine." Joseph walked back to the bed of the wagon and drew aside a pile of woolen blankets to reveal Killy McBride, who'd fought with them through all five years of the war, lying there still and pale.

The wiry Irishman didn't move or open his eyes.

"Is he dead?" Connor and Iain asked almost as one.

"Dead drunk." Joseph reached in, grabbed Killy by the wrist and drew him to a sitting position, the motion jarring Killy to confused wakefulness. "I found him in the streets. He'd been thrown out of White Horse Tavern for failing to pay for his rum."

Killy glanced about. "Hildie, my love?"

Joseph glared at Killy, then tossed him over his shoulder like a sack of potatoes. "He's senseless. The wagon and horse are his."

Iain and Connor shared another glance.

"Hildie?" Connor asked.

"Gundhilda Janssen." Joseph strode toward the house, Killy hanging over his shoulder. "She's the owner of the White Horse Tavern."

Connor followed after Joseph, Iain behind him. "The big Dutchwoman who nearly gelded Brandon when she caught him eyein' her paps?"

"Aye," Joseph called back. "Killy has lost his heart to her."

"Miss Janssen?" Connor could scarce believe it. He glanced back at Iain. "Och, she's fair enough, I suppose, but she's near as tall as I am."

The top of Killy's head didn't even reach Connor's shoulder.

Iain grinned. "Aye, and she has a temper."

The cabin's door opened.

Annie, Iain's wife, stood on its threshold, worry on her pretty face. "Is he sick?"

"He's sufferin' from the bite of the bottle," Iain answered. "Joseph found him lying in the street in Albany."

"Bring him inside afore he catches his death." Annie stood back to let Joseph pass. "Oh, Killy. What have you done to yourself now?"

With Killy safely in Annie's care and the first of the morning chores done, Connor slipped quietly away.

The sun was good and up before Connor reached the old oak. It grew near the burnie that marked the western edge of their lands, the water now turned to hard ice. There, on a thick, gnarled branch, he spotted what he'd come for — mistletoe. Its green leaves and waxy white berries stood out against the rough, gray bark.

The priests and old women of Skye, where Connor and his brothers had been born, held mistletoe to be sacred. Green when other plants had died, mistletoe was said to be twice as powerful if it grew upon an oak. When hung above doorways, it kept evil at bay, blessing all who passed beneath it. And lads and lasses who kissed beneath it could be assured they would marry in the new year.

Connor wanted this to be a good Christmas for them all, for it was their first Yule since war's ending, the first time the three brothers would be home, all of them together with their wives. He could not wait to surprise Sarah with the gold wedding band he'd bought for her, could not wait to slip it onto her finger. He wanted nothing to spoil the joy of the holiday for her.

Aye, the discord between Morgan and Amalie must end. Connor didn't know if the stories about mistletoe were true, but if it could help unmarried lads and lasses to wed, perhaps it could mend hurts between a husband and wife.

He kicked off his snowshoes and began to climb.

Annie poured a cup of willow bark tea and handed it carefully to Killy, who was now awake and sober enough to sit up on the pallet the men had made for him in front of the sitting room hearth. "'Tis bitter, but it will help soothe your aching head."

Wincing at the sound of her voice, Killy accepted the tin cup. "Have you anything stronger — a little hair of the dog?"

She narrowed her eyes and frowned at him. "Nay, you're no' fittin' to be at the rum. Now drink your tea."

In truth, it worried her to see him in this state — suffering from drink, thinner, pale. She'd always had a soft place for him in her heart. He would certainly attribute this to what he called his "Irish charm," and he *had* stood out as one of a handful of Irishmen in MacKinnon's Rangers, a fighting force organized by Iain that had been made mostly of towering Highland Scots. But Annie thought her affection for him came in part because he'd been one of the first of Iain's Rangers to be kind to her — and in part because she'd spent long days and nights tending him when he'd been wounded in battle.

The poor man's scars proved that he'd lived a rough life—the garroting scar on his throat from the time the English had tried to hang him; dozens of scars on his face and hands from cuts, knife wounds, and graze marks from lead balls; and upon his head, beneath the blue Scotch bonnet he always wore, the patch of puckered, colorless flesh where he'd been scalped and left for dead.

Killy had nine lives, for certain, but it seemed to Annie that he was running out.

He grimaced as he drank, then handed her the cup, shuddering. "I'd just as soon drink my own piss as ... Pardon me, ma'am."

She ignored his crude words, filling the cup with cold water and handing it back to him. "Drink. 'Tis only water."

He drank — then held out the cup for more.

She filled it again.

Downstairs, Amalie and Sarah were making Joseph a late breakfast and trading news with him, while he acquainted himself with little William. Iain was seeing to chores with Connor and Morgan. And Annie realized this might be the only chance she had to speak with Killy alone.

"Joseph tells us he found you in the streets. He says a passerby told him you were thrown out of a tavern because you could not pay. How did you come to be in such a state, Killy — and just a week afore Christmas?"

His scarred face turned red with anger — and then crumpled. Chin wobbling, he looked up at her. "It's for love's sake that I'm cast down."

So Killy had fallen in love.

"Who is she?" Annie took the cup and sat on a stool beside him.

"Gundhilda Janssen, the proprietress of the White Horse."

"The White Horse?"

"A public house, ma'am — a tavern." Killy's face was transformed by a dreamy smile. "She is fair with yellow hair and bright blue eyes. She is buxom, too, aye, and strong. When she's angry, her face comes alive. I've watched her toss grown men out on their arses, so I have."

Annie fought not to smile at this colorful description. "You wish to marry her?"

"Aye, I do."

"Does Miss Janssen no' return your favor?"

Killy's gaze dropped to the floor. "I cannot say."

"Have you no' spoken wi' her or asked her father for permission to court her?"

"Her father is gone from this world. She has a younger brother who does her biddin', so it is her favor I must win." His blue eyes filled with despair. "I've spoken winsome words to her, but she tells me I'm too far gone with drink to mean them and calls me a silver-tongued Irish devil. When I'm near her, I become a witless coward."

Annie fought back a smile. "You're a Ranger, Killy, one of my husband's most-trusted men. I've seen you laugh and jest in battle. You're no' lackin' for courage. Surely it must be more terrifyin' to face the enemy than to speak wi' a lass — "

"Pardon me for sayin' so, but you know naught of it." Killy's smile vanished. "A woman must only say 'aye' or 'nay' to a suitor, while a man must win her heart or find himself rejected and without hope."

Annie supposed Killy was right. She'd never been in the position of trying to win a man's affection. Iain had not courted her in any traditional way, their love for one another taking them both by surprise.

"When you return to Albany, you must convince her that what you feel for her is true by speakin' with her when you're off the drink. It would be better for you to ken where her heart lies than to pine away for her."

The stubborn Irishman shook his head. "'Twould be a fool's errand. She could never love a penniless, battle-scarred old carcass like me."

Annie could tell that he truly believed this. "And so you drank your last shilling."

"It wasn't so much rum as you might be thinkin'." He gave a chuckle, then frowned. "Oh, aye, it was. But it might have been more had I been paid. The Crown hasn't yet seen fit to pay any of us Rangers for last summer's campaigns."

"How can that be?"

"Haviland says we Rangers fought on behalf of the Colonies, not for that bastard King George. Er ... Pardon me, ma'am."

But Annie scarce noticed the insult to her sovereign, stunned as she was to think that Brigadier General Haviland had refused to pay the very men whose sweat and blood had helped the British to win the accursed war. That must be why Killy was so thin. He likely hadn't had a good meal in months.

And the other Rangers? Some had families, children to feed.

"Does my husband ken this, Killy?"

CHAPTER TWO

Iain jabbed at the embers in the bedroom fireplace, his anger as hot as the blaze. He fought not to shout lest he wake the bairns, his words coming out in a gruff whisper. "By God, 'tis an outrage! Those men risked their lives for Britain, sufferin' hardships Haviland cannae imagine, and now the *mac dìolain* refuses to pay them? The bastard hasn't a shred of honor!"

Iain had spent much of the evening discussing Killy's news with his brothers, and they had decided to leave for Albany in the morning to take up the matter with Haviland in person, while Joseph and Killy stayed to watch over the women and children. Though Iain hated to leave home so close to Christmastide, neither he nor his brothers could abide the notion that the men who'd fought under the MacKinnon name for five long years should be denied their due and made to suffer want, especially at Christmas when lack was so keenly felt.

"Do you think Haviland will listen to you?" Wearing only her shift, a shawl around her shoulders, Annie sat in the rocking chair, brushing her long hair, the flaxen strands gleaming like gold in the firelight. "If he has no honor, what is to stop him from clappin' the three of you in irons?"

She spoke the words calmly, but Iain could sense her fear. Her worries were not just fretful imaginings.

'Twas a journey to Albany almost six years past that had started all of this. Wentworth had watched Iain fight a man who'd been about to kill a whore he'd used but didn't wish to pay. Impressed by Iain's skill, Wentworth had taken Iain and his brothers prisoner on false murder charges. He'd given Iain a choice between being hanged together with his brothers or fighting for the British as the commander of a ranging company. Not wishing to see his brothers die for naught, Iain had chosen the latter.

He put more wood on the fire, then turned to his wife. "Haviland cannae press us into service, if that is what you fear. The war is over."

"That doesna mean he willna find upon some other treachery. You ken as well as I that he doesna care for you or the Rangers." Her strokes grew agitated, her hand gripping her silver-handled hairbrush tightly.

"Come, *mo leannan*. I willna allow harm to befall us." Iain took the brush from her hand, set it aside, and drew her onto her feet and into his embrace. He held her tight, kissed her hair, the feel of her precious in his arms. His gaze traveled from little Mara, who would soon be one year old, to Iain Cameron, soon to be two, and he silently cursed Haviland again. "I hate to be leavin' you and the bairns so near to Christmas, but I must."

Annie looked up at him, cupped his cheek with her palm, understanding in her eyes, a soft smile on her lips. "I knew you'd be goin' the moment Killy told me. If there's augh' you can do to right this wrong, you *must* go. Your men are as kin to us. Their troubles are our troubles."

Iain looked into the eyes of the woman he loved and wondered not for the first time how he'd been so lucky as to win her for himself. "If only I'd known sooner, this would already be behind us."

Why had the men not told him?

Killy said the men thought Iain and his brothers already knew. But, although it was true that neither Connor nor Iain had received a farthing for last summer's campaigns, they'd thought little of it. For one, they had no need of the coin, the farm more than prosperous enough to sustain the three brothers and their families. For another, Connor had spent part of the campaign season in irons, while Iain had been pressed back into service after the campaigns had already begun. They had assumed that Wentworth had cut off Connor's pay and hadn't had time to place Iain on the rolls before the Wyandot had taken him captive.

"Let us pray that all will quickly be set to rights and you'll be safely home by Christmas Eve." She turned her head to the side, rested her cheek against his chest, her slender arms holding him close.

He tucked a finger beneath her chin, ducked down, and brushed his lips over hers. "Will you send me away wi' a proper farewell, wife?"

A smile tugged at her lips. "But Killy and Joseph are sleepin' in the next room, and the children…"

He slid his fingers into her hair. "Then you'd best no' scream, aye?"

His mouth closed over hers, and they kissed long and slow, desire rising in a rush of heat as their tongues curled together. He felt Annie's nimble fingers unbuttoning his shirt and reached down to untie the fall of his breeches. Because of Annie's monthly, it had been at least a week since they'd taken their pleasure together, and he was as eager for her as she was for him.

He broke the kiss, let his shirt fall to the floor, shucked his breeches and moccasins, watching while Annie walked to the bed, her movements seductive. She turned to face him, lifted her chemise over her head, and let it fall, baring herself to his gaze, a smile that promised paradise on her lips.

"My sweet Annie." His cock was already hard, standing against his belly, the heat in his blood leaving him radgie. He closed the distance between them caught her in his arms, and kissed her as they sank to the bearskin together in a tangle of limbs. His hands were upon her and hers on him, seeking, stroking, rousing one another, their urgency growing with each shared breath.

They'd been wed more than two years now, and Iain was more in love with her, more in *lust* with her, than he'd been when he'd taken her to wife. The blazing passion of their first months together had given way to a deep, slow burn that needed but the merest touch to burst into flame. And those flames consumed him now.

Pulse pounding, he kissed and tasted her, teasing her breasts with his tongue, drawing her nipples to tight peaks with his lips, one hand busy between her thighs, stroking her where she was most sensitive. Her quiet whimpers and sighs heightened his arousal, her wetness proof of her need.

He raised himself above her, settled himself between her parted thighs, and for a moment he let his gaze move over her, in awe of her body and what it could do. Not only did she bring him great pleasure, but she had also given life to his children. Aye, motherhood had changed her, but only in ways that made her more desirable. Her breasts were larger, her hips more womanly. There were also faint silver lines on the soft curve of her belly. Though Annie had at first feared they would dampen his desire for her, those lines only made him want her more. For like the blue designs etched into the skin of his arms that had heralded his arrival into manhood, they were her warrior marks — proof of the pain she had endured for the love of him.

She was beauty. She was joy. She was life.

God's blood, he loved her.

He slid inside her with a single, slow thrust, her slick quim hot and tight around him. With slow, steady strokes, he bent his mind and body to her pleasure, the sweet distress on her face filling him with a sense of satisfaction as her need grew more desperate, her nails digging into the skin of his back, her hips rising to meet his thrusts, her pulse pounding beneath his lips. With a soft whimper, she arched off the bed, clinging to him as she came, her body trembling.

"*Mo leannan.*" He whispered endearments against her skin, his heart soaring to see the bliss upon her face.

And then he, too, claimed his peak, losing himself inside her.

They left just after dawn, trudging through deep snows in their bearskin coats, snowshoes strapped to their thick winter moccasins. It was faster to walk than to try to drive a wagon. There were no wheels to get stuck in drifts or break on ice, and the exertion kept them warm.

It reminded Morgan of his days as a Ranger — walking with his brothers through the forest, tumpline pack upon his back, a rifled musket beneath his arm. It felt good to exert himself, physical toil helping to release his anger and frustration. But even the sight of the forest blanketed in snow did not lift his spirits.

He and Amalie had slept apart again last night. He'd gone to bed to find her asleep on a pallet in the next room near their twin sons' cradles. Enraged to see her thus, he'd awoken her and demanded she return to their bed.

He was only trying to protect her, but that's not how she saw it. "Do you not want me, Morgan? Do you feel no desire for me?"

He'd tried again to explain. "I love you, Amalie, and wish only to spare you sufferin'. We've two strong sons, and I'll ask no more from you. I willna risk you in childbirth again, nor would I see our sons grow up motherless."

"You cannot make that choice for me. You are acting out of selfishness and wish only to free yourself from fear. Where is your faith, Morgan?"

He'd lost his temper then. "Your years in the convent have blinded you to the harshness of this life."

Tears had filled her eyes. "If I cannot lie with you as your wife, I will not lie with you at all."

When he'd realized that nothing he could say would coax her beneath the bearskin again, he'd offered her the bed and had slept on the floor himself. It had been a cold and lonely night and had been followed by a colder morning — and a hard parting.

Amalie had seen him off as any good wife would, making certain he had food aplenty for the journey. But there had been no joy in her eyes, only sadness. "God go with you, Morgan. Be safe."

It felt wrong to leave her now. Everything inside him wanted to turn and head back to the cabin, the discord between them leaving a heaviness inside him that nothing save the resolution of their troubles could dispel. And yet he had a shared duty toward the men who had fought so hard under the MacKinnon name during the war. His own troubles would have to wait.

Perhaps when he was in Albany, he could find a gift fitting for her, some way to prove to her that he *did* love her, no matter what she might believe.

They reached Albany just before sunset, entering through the southwestern gate near the river, turning left at the Dutch Reformed Church and walking up Jonker Street toward the British garrison on the hill above town. They passed the chandler, the butcher, two bakers, and Oldiah Cooper's tavern where they'd often quenched their thirst.

Connor had always liked Albany with its busy streets and shops. Some of the doorways they passed were decorated with pine garlands — surely the homes and establishments of the city's Dutch inhabitants, who had already celebrated St. Nicholas's Day with their Sinterklaas, who, their legends told, arrived by ship bearing gifts for children. 'Twas a strange tradition, though Connor would never say so to a Dutchman.

Most people were indoors enjoying the warmth of their fires and a good meal, their day's work done. Others hurried by, huddling deeper in their coats for warmth. Some watched Connor and his brothers pass by, recognition on their faces.

The MacKinnon brothers were well known here.

They reached the garrison, entered the gate, and made their way toward Haviland's headquarters, where they found two young redcoats standing guard and shivering at the door.

It felt to Iain, as the eldest, to speak for the three of them. "I'm Iain MacKinnon. These are my brothers. We're here to speak wi' Haviland."

The lads' eyes went wide, surprise and a hint of fear on their faces.

One of them found his tongue. "Is the Brigadier General expectin' you?"

"Nay, but he will speak wi' us just the same," Iain answered.

The lads looked at one another, and then the one who'd spoken turned, opened the door, and dashed inside.

Iain switched to Gaelic. "I fear we've arrived too late in the day. 'Tis likely Haviland is fillin' his belly and will refuse to see us."

"You're no' thinkin' of forcin' our way past his guard, are you?" Morgan asked.

Connor would stand beside Iain if that was his plan, though he thought it unwise. "'Tis a sure way to find ourselves in the guardhouse."

"I've no desire to spend Yule in chains. If he willna see us now, we'll come back in the morn' — and every morn' until he does."

It was not long before the young redcoat returned. Judging from the new look of contempt on his face, Haviland had shared his loathing of the Rangers with the lad. Like far too many of his ilk, Haviland couldn't abide the thought that mere Colonials might know more about fighting and surviving in the wilderness than trained British troops. But the Rangers and Colonial militias had more than proved their worth in the winning of the war, and no amount of disregard from Haviland or his men could change that.

The lad looked down his nose at them. "The Brigadier General is dining with his guests and cannot be bothered by the likes of you just now. He says to come back at ten sharp in the morning."

Well, that was something.

Iain looked into the lad's eyes until the boy began to squirm, likely regretting the haughty tone he'd taken. "Ten sharp then."

They turned and headed back down Jonker Street with naught left to do but make their way to the White Horse Tavern, where they had business with the buxom proprietress — and where they might get warm food and a room for the night.

They found the place on Pearl Street, Connor following his brothers through the thick oaken door. Warmth hit him in the face, followed by the delicious scents of roasted meats, baking bread, spices, pipe smoke, and ale. The public rooms were well lighted, fat candles burning on each table, in sconces on the walls, and in iron chandeliers that hung from the oaken ceiling.

His stomach growled. "I swear I could eat an entire bullock myself."

"You'll have to fight me for it," Morgan muttered.

They made their way toward a table near the fireplace, people staring at them and breaking into excited whispers.

"That's the MacKinnon brothers as I live and breathe! If not for them, we'd all be speakin' French today."

"I hear they're exiled Jacobites who ate the flesh of their dead."

"They taught the French a lesson or two, so they did."

Like his brothers, Connor ignored these mutterings, slipping out of his gear and bearskin coat, and taking his seat on the wooden bench beside Morgan, his hand moving of its own accord to make sure the letter Sarah had written to Wentworth was still safe and dry in his shirt pocket.

"If you should happen upon him..." she'd said, clearly hoping they would find him at the fort.

"We dinnae ken that he is there. He might have boarded a ship and be well on his way to New York. Even if he is in Albany, we cannae be certain he will speak wi' us." At the crestfallen expression on her face, Connor had softened his words. "I'll do all I can to see that he gets this. I promise."

Keeping that promise would mean checking Wentworth's old residence on Market Street, as well as every inn in town, not to mention the garrison.

"Is that she?" Iain spoke in Gaelic, his gaze fixed on someone behind them.

Connor glanced over his shoulder to see a tall woman wearing a plain blue gown and white apron and carrying four pints of ale in big, strong hands. She was not plump, nor was she thin, her frame large, her bosom and hips full and rounded. Her flaxen hair was braided and piled neatly upon her head like a crown, her cheeks flushed from exertion. "Aye. 'Tis Gundhilda."

The three brothers shared a glance, all of them fighting not to smile, an image in their minds of tough little Killy courting a woman who could, in all likelihood, pick him up and throw him.

And yet...

Morgan said it first. "She is fair of face, and her bosom..."

Connor nodded. "Aye. Her bosom."

'Twas she who came to their table.

She glared down at them, but behind the anger, Connor saw something akin to hurt in her blue eyes, as if she knew they'd been talking about her — as if men always talked and tittled about her. From what he knew, she'd inherited the tavern from her father, as her brother was too weak-minded to run it himself. 'Twould be rough on a lass to be the proprietress of an alehouse.

"Tonight, we've shepherd's pie with mutton and a pheasant stew." Her words were spoken with a faint Dutch accent he found charming.

"We've a small matter to discuss wi' you afore we dine, Miss Janssen." Iain drew out his leather coin purse. "I'm Iain MacKinnon. These are my brothers, Morgan and Connor. We've come on behalf of Killy McBride to settle his debt to you."

CHAPTER THREE

Hildie Janssen looked down at the three MacKinnon brothers. Did they truly believe she didn't know who they were? There was no one in Albany who did not know of them and their deeds in the war. They were easily recognizable with their long dark hair and Indian markings. All three of them were big men, taller even than she, their arms thick, their shoulders broad.

Ja, they were handsome men. Even she could see that.

But, in the end, that's all they were — men.

She frowned. "Why does Killy not come himself?"

Not that she wished to see him again. He'd sat here under her roof drinking her rum and doing his best to make a laughingstock of her.

Iain MacKinnon glanced quickly at his brothers. "He, um…"

The youngest brother, Connor, spoke quickly. "He's sick, miss."

"Sick with drink, I'd wager." Hildie was no fool.

She had grown up in her father's *bierhal* and had been serving ale to men just like the MacKinnon brothers since she was a girl of ten. She'd heard what men said about women when they'd filled their bellies with rum. She'd felt the unwelcome burn of their leering glances and had had to fight off their groping hands since she'd first begun to develop breasts.

She'd listened to their sweet words, only to have those words turn sour the moment they realized she wouldn't lift her skirts for them. She'd learned at a young age how to protect herself, breaking more than a few wayward fingers, grabbing men who touched her by the stones and leading them by their cods to the door.

Now that she was thirty and five, well beyond marriageable age, men spoke sweet words only when they wanted to humiliate her, laughing as they tried to outdo one another with false praise for prettiness she no longer possessed. She knew she was not fair, nor even feminine. She was so much taller and bigger than most women, bigger even than many men, her face plain, her hair beginning to turn silver.

Even so, it hurt to be mocked. And, although her age and appearance made her the butt of men's jests, that didn't stop them from trying to get into her bed. The more they drank, the more they professed to love her, the strength of their passion for her a measure of how much they'd had to drink.

Apart from her brother, Bram, she had no use for men.

Killy was the worst of them, sitting at her tables night after night, drinking her finest rum, speaking sweetly to her with his Irish lilt, making her dream of things that could never be. He was older and shorter than she, but he was handsome enough, his skin browned by the sun, the scars on his face giving him a rugged, devilish look she rather liked. She knew he'd earned most of those scars in the fighting with MacKinnon's Rangers. She'd thought of him as a hero — until he'd begun to taunt her with poetry and nonsensical flattery. He'd meant none of what he'd said, but had merely been drunk and lonely for the pleasures of a woman's company.

"Nay, miss," the youngest brother objected. "Killy was driven to drink only because he is heartsick for fear he has displeased you. He feels great affection for you."

Hildie felt blood rush into her cheeks, the hurt inside her quickly swallowed by anger. They were teasing her, joining with Killy in a shared jest about her. But she would not allow them to mock her in her own tavern. "That Irish devil! You will stop your teasing now, or I'll have Bram come and throw you into the snow. I'd have thought the three of you more honorable than this."

The brothers looked at each other, blank expressions on their faces.

"Have we given you offense, miss?" Iain MacKinnon looked confused.

"Do not think to taunt me, for I'll not be having it — not here, under my own roof. I've no use for men's drunken flattery and lies. If you wish to settle Killy's debt, that will be one shilling six."

The brothers gaped at each other.

"One shilling six pence?" the youngest said, looking for a moment like he might rise to his feet. "How bloody much rum did that bast — "

The middle brother restrained him.

"One shilling six it is." Iain MacKinnon opened the coin purse, counted out the coins, and placed them one at a time in Hildie's upturned palm. "He'd have paid it himself, but Haviland has not given him his wages for last summer's campaigns. None of my men have been paid."

Hildie was not surprised. She'd had more than one British officer bring his men in for food and drink and pay not a farthing for it.

The elder brother finished counting out the coins. "And that settles his accounts?"

"*Ja.*" She ran a finger over the coins, counting. "What will you have tonight?"

Iain MacKinnon answered. "We'll have both the shepherd's pie and the pheasant stew. Bring plenty of bread and butter, too, and ale for the three of us."

Big men made for big appetites.

She closed her fist around the coins, gave them a nod, and turned toward the kitchens, only to find Connor MacKinnon following her.

He stopped her. "Miss Janssen, 'tis sorry I am if we left you feelin' unsettled in any way, but we dinnae lie or jest wi' you. Killy is undone by his affection for you."

"Bram!" Hildie shouted for her brother, who was carrying firewood in from the woodpile. "I'll have you thrown out, MacKinnon!"

But MacKinnon was not cowed. "He told my sister-by-marriage that he is cast down for the love of you and would ask you to marry him if he thought you'd consent."

She felt her fist clench, the humiliation of having a man everyone in Albany knew and admired torment her like this almost more than she could bear.

MacKinnon held up his hands in a gesture of surrender. "I swear to you on my honor as a Scotsman and a MacKinnon that I'm no' jestin' or deceivin' you."

Hildie stared at the big Scotsman, unable to believe him and yet certain he would not swear such a thing on his honor unless it was true. But how could that be? "Killy truly spoke those words?"

"Aye, so he did."

"He…he was not drunk?"

"Nay, miss. He was on the hurtin' side of the bottle, if you ken my meanin'. What man would lie about such a thing with a poundin' head?"

Before she could think on this, MacKinnon drew something out of his pocket and held it out for her. It was a plant of some kind.

"'Tis mistletoe." He gave it to her. "'Tis said to possess magic. We believe that if a man and woman kiss beneath mistletoe at Christmas, they'll wed in the new year. I bring it as a token of Killy's affections."

Killy had sent this for her?

Hildie stared at it. She heard what MacKinnon said, but her mind could scarcely fathom it. Could all of Killy's absurd, outlandish, sweet words have been sincere?

Sarah sat with Annie and Amalie, sharing their memories of Christmas while they stitched gifts for the men, taking advantage of their husbands' journey to Albany to sew, knit, and embroider without fear of being caught and ruining their Christmas surprises. Cups of hot tea and Annie's delicious shortbread sat on the table before them. Miraculously, the babies were all asleep. Iain Cameron played with wooden horses on the floor. Artair and Beatan, Iain's enormous wolfhounds, dozed on the braided rug near the door as if keeping guard. Killy and Joseph were in the barn seeing to the heavy chores.

"After Mass, we lit candles and placed them in the windows, then set food and drink on the table in case the Virgin should call upon us during the night," Amalie said, speaking of her life in the Ursuline convent at Trois-Rivières, where she'd been raised. "I cannot say for certain, but I believe the Mother Superior enjoyed an extra meal and glass of wine on Christmas Eve."

Sarah laughed, amused by the unlikely image of a stern nun drinking wine on Christmas Eve, the warm winter hat she'd begun knitting for Killy slowly taking shape in her hands.

"In my great-great-grandfather's time, we didna celebrate Christmas in Scotland. 'Twas forbidden. But that has changed." Annie's voice took on a wistful tone. "When I was a child, we hung garlands of holly and pine on the banisters, above the hearths, and around the doors and windows. I can still smell it, so fresh and clean, wi' shortcake bakin' in the kitchen..."

Sarah's heart ached for Annie, for her family was gone, her brothers and fathers slain by Highland Scots at Prestonpans, her mother murdered. Now Annie was the only one who remembered those days. "You must miss them terribly."

There was a sheen of tears in Annie's eyes, but she smiled, her delicate stitches not faltering. "Aye, I do, especially at Christmastide."

Sarah was surprised to realize she didn't miss her family at all.

You are with your true family now.

Her marriage to Connor had been the beginning of a new life for her, far from the dreariness and loneliness that had been her existence before scandal had compelled her father to send her to the Colonies. Annie and Amalie were more like sisters to her than her four sisters back home, Iain, Morgan, and Joseph the brothers she'd never had.

And Connor...

She loved him more than she'd thought it was possible to love anyone. He had given her so much — his protection, his love, a son — and now she would give him something in return. She had arranged such surprises for him and for her new family that waiting for Christmas was proving to be most difficult, the anticipation almost more than she could bear. On the morning of Christmas Eve, her gifts for the family would arrive. She could scarce wait to see everyone's faces.

How strange it was to think that she hadn't known them last Christmas. Now she was one of them.

She glanced down at little William, who slept bundled in a blanket on a pallet of furs beside her yarn basket.

"But what of your memories, Sarah?" Amalie asked. "Christmas must have been splendid at the British court."

"My mother could not bear to be at court and only went when summoned by my grandmother." Her mother, a very strict Lutheran, had found the merriment surrounding Christmas to be sinful. "We spent Christmastide at my father's estate outside London. Servants decorated with pine boughs, holly, and candles, but what I loved most was the music. They played the grandest music at church, and we all sang together."

"And so shall we," Amalie said with a bright smile. "I do so love your playing."

"Thank you." Sarah felt a rush of joy — and anticipation.

Music had always been her great passion, a passion her mother had tried to squelch. Sarah's desire to play for more than the thirty minutes a day her mother had allowed her had led to scandal that had gotten her exiled to the Colonies. But how blessed Sarah was now to be the wife of a man who encouraged her to play, to be part of a family that enjoyed her music. She still couldn't believe Connor and his brothers had brought her harpsichord, a gift from Uncle William, all the way from Fort Edward to the farm.

And it came to her that there was more good cheer and Christmas spirit in this family made up of people who ought to have been enemies —

Protestants and Catholics, English and French, Jacobites and loyalists —
than there had been in her parents' wealthy and well-ordered home.

Then she asked the question some part of her had been wanting to ask
for weeks. "Does it trouble either of you to spend these sacred days with
people who do not fully share your faith?"

Amalie looked up from her needlework. "It is easier for me than it
must be for the two of you. My husband and I are both Catholic. It does not
upset me that you and Annie are Protestant. That is part of who you are,
and I love you both."

Amalie's answer was as gracious as Sarah had known it would be.

Annie set her sewing in her lap. "I spent my first Christmas Eve as
Iain's wife alone in the cabin on Ranger Island, while he went to Mass wi'
Father Delavay. Then I realized my children would be raised as Catholics.
If I didna join in, my husband would be deprived of his wife's company
and my children would grow up confused. Now I pray beside him. I have
faith that I am meant to be wi' Iain, and that is enough for me."

Annie made it all seem so simple.

Sarah found herself smiling. "We *shall* have a merry Christmas, shall
we not?"

As long as Connor and his brothers made it safely home from Albany
in time, this would be Sarah's happiest Christmas ever.

Morgan and his brothers bided the night in one of the upstairs rooms
that Miss Janssen let out to travelers. The fire was warm, even if
the room itself was crowded with other men. They woke early the next
morning as was their wont and broke their fast together below stairs,

sharing a salver of warm bread, cheeses, and sausage and washing that down with ale and cups of hot coffee.

Morgan ate quickly then bade Iain and Connor to take their time. "I've a matter to see to in town. I'll be back afore it's time to meet wi' Haviland."

Leaving his pack with his brothers, he slipped his coin purse into the pocket of his bearskin coat and walked out onto Albany's snowy streets. The cold snatched his breath away, the sun still sitting low in the sky, its weak rays peeking through a break in the clouds. Wood smoke lingered in the air, mingling with the scent of freshly baked bread. It was still early enough that the streets weren't yet busy, a wagon trundling by with a load of timber, a blacksmith's hammer ringing against its anvil somewhere in the distance.

Morgan made his way through the streets looking for he knew not what. He came upon the bookbinder and was tempted to enter, but he'd already bought Amalie a new book for Christmas. He wanted to give her something more, something that would prove to her what he seemed to be unable to prove — that he loved her.

He crossed the street when he spied a seamstress' shop, only to find it was not yet open, the door locked, the windows dark. He huddled deeper in his bearskin coat and went on his way until he came upon a mercantile, its window displaying goods from garments to wooden toy soldiers to cook pots. He nudged the door open, the jingling of a bell announcing his arrival.

Warmth rushed against his skin, a fire burning in one of those Franklin stoves against the far wall. The front room was a riot of colors, objects, and scents — wood smoke, rose soap, leather, spices, linen.

He wiped his feet on the mat, glancing about. Bolts of cloth. Ribbons. Tatted lace. Dyed yarn. Coffeepots and teapots. Teacups and saucers. Pots and pans. Dolls and toy swords. Parchment and ink. Shoes and woolen socks. Clothing and blankets. Caps and hats of all kinds. Coffee and candy. Soaps and salves.

The sound of voices came from the back — a woman speaking Dutch, a man answering. Then an older woman stepped out from the back. Tall and well dressed with a ruffled bonnet covering her gray hair, she greeted him warmly, her eyes widening almost imperceptibly when she saw him. "May I help you find something, Mr. MacKinnon?"

He was accustomed to being recognized and gave it little thought.

"Aye, madam, and thank you." But Morgan wasn't sure what he wanted. "I'm searchin' for a gift for my wife, somethin' special."

He found himself telling the woman about Amalie — her sweetness, her quick mind, her love of reading, her beautiful long hair. "She has endured much for my sake, leavin' the world she knew for mine, forsakin' her own people to be at my side, endurin' a fearsome travail to bear me twins."

The matron's lips curved in a smile. "Twins?"

"Aye." Morgan couldn't help but smile back. "Sons."

And then he realized that he'd been rambling on about Amalie to a stranger. "Forgi' me, madam. 'Tis unseemly to be speakin' of my wife thus."

The matron gave a nod of her head, her gaze warm, a faint smile still on her lips, and Morgan knew she did not hold his lapse against him. "What do you think she might like? We have chocolates, small bars of scented soap, ribbons."

But Morgan wanted to get Amalie something much finer than candy, soap, or ribbons. Unshaven, wearing moccasins and his bearskin coat, he must surely seem like a man without a farthing to his name. "I'm not a poor man. I've some coin."

The matron turned and picked up a tray that sat on a shelf behind the counter. "We have a few silver rings, this lovely silver locket in the shape of a heart, and this brooch with garnets."

Morgan studied each item, trying not to show his surprise when he saw that the brooch cost five pounds. He could buy a fine sword with that sum. And as he gazed at the polished silver and glittering garnets, he knew that none of these fine things would matter to Amalie. "My wife cares not at all for such finery — nor can I be spendin' quite such a sum. I've at most a shilling fifteen in my purse."

His stomach sank. There was naught for Amalie here.

Then his gaze fell on a pair of combs. They seemed to be made of polished bone, tiny flowers and leaves carved out of the fan-shaped handles. An image came into his mind of Amalie brushing her dark hair, piling it atop her head, and holding it in place with these combs. "May I see those?"

He knew they were most certainly beyond what he could afford, but the image in his mind remained.

"Certainly." The matron placed them on the wooden counter before Morgan. "They are carved from ivory and were bought from the wife of a captain who sails with the East India Company. He acquired them for her on his travels."

They were beautiful, delicate, much more modest than the locket or the jeweled brooch. "These are lovely, but surely they are beyond my means."

"These combs are just the price you were seeking," the matron said, removing a small slip of paper from the back of one of the combs and crumpling it in her fingers. "They are one shilling ten."

"One shilling ten?" A good musket, a knife, a bottle of rum — those prices he knew well, but the cost of jewelry or ivory combs? He grinned, thrust his hand into his pocket, seeking his coin purse. "I'd be most grateful if you could wrap those, madam. Och, they will look bonnie in my wife's hair."

He left the merchant ten minutes later, the combs safe in a bag of crimson velvet and tucked deeply in his pocket. He was so pleased with his purchase that he didn't notice how the matron watched him from the store window, a smile on her face, a wistful look in her eyes.

CHAPTER FOUR

Iain stood with his brothers outside Haviland's study, his temper growing darker by the moment. "He bade us be here at ten," he said to his brothers in Gaelic. "'Tis now past eleven, and still he refuses to admit us."

"It pleases him to make us wait." Connor leaned back in his chair and stretched out his legs. "The man is a *neach dìolain.*"

A true bastard.

"Aye, that he is."

Iain strode to the window, looked out on the parade ground. A party of Indians — Mohawk traders by the look of them — came to the gates of the fort, but were turned away. Two errand boys stood close beside the blacksmith's shop, no doubt trying to keep warm. Redcoats walked here and there, huddled in their winter coats. Many of them would be returning to war soon, for although the peace was won here in the Colonies, the war between France and England and their allies was not over.

Iain thanked God every day that he and his brothers were out of the fray — and had survived. So many good men had not.

Time dragged on slowly until it was almost the noon hour and Iain's stomach began to complain. Then the door opened.

A young lieutenant appeared. "Brigadier General Haviland will see you now."

"Is that so? Och, well, we wouldna want to keep Haviland waitin', now would we boys?" Iain started forward.

The lieutenant blocked his path, holding out his hand. "I have orders that you are not to enter armed. You must leave your weapons here."

Iain's already bad temper flashed hot. "Does he mean to insult us? We fought wi' him this past summer, and now he treats us as enemies?"

Fear passed over the lad's face. "I...I know only that I have been told not to let you enter still armed."

"I dinnae like the feel of this." Iain spoke in Gaelic and knew his brothers shared his misgivings. Then he switched to English again and made a show of conceding. "Och, for Satan! Very well."

He dropped his tumpline pack, drew out his sword and hunting knife and piled them, together with his musket and pistol, in the surprised lieutenant's arms. Following his example, Morgan and Connor did the same, until the lad was weighed down by heavy steel. But Iain did not hand over the knife he kept secreted inside his leggings, nor did his brothers reveal theirs.

If Haviland tried to detain them...

Iain pushed past the lieutenant and walked down the hallway, Connor's voice following him.

"I dinnae ken what Haviland seeks to gain from this. If we had a mind to go after him wi' our blades, lad, neither you nor a dozen like you could stop us. Mind how you hold that, aye? Are you tryin' to cut off a finger?"

They walked down the hallway toward another closed door where two more redcoats stood guard. One of them turned, opened the door, bowed. "They are here, sir."

Iain entered to find Haviland sitting at Wentworth's old writing table, powdered wig upon his head, his uniform immaculate. He did not stand, but peered at Iain and his brothers through narrowed eyes, disdain on his face. "You wished to see me, MacKinnon? What is it you want?"

Iain had never been one for pleasantries and was glad to get to the heart of the matter. "The men have no' been paid what they're owed for this past summer's campaigns."

'Twas strange to see another sitting in the position Wentworth had once held — and even stranger for Iain to find himself wishing that the man before him were Wentworth. He didn't trust Haviland.

"You speak of your Rangers?" Haviland's voice held a note of contempt.

"Aye. They've no' been paid for their service."

Haviland looked confused. "But why come to me?"

Was the man a simpleton?

"You've taken Wentworth's command, aye?" Iain asked. "Payin' the Rangers fell to him according to our arrangement. Now that task falls to you."

"I am aware of no such arrangement. Do you have proof of this?"

Iain looked over at his brothers, saw the disbelief he felt mirrored on their faces. "'Twas a gentleman's agreement, each of us givin' and keepin' our word. Surely, there must be records, ledgers, an accountin' of what was paid—"

"I've seen no ledgers, nor did I read anything in Brigadier General Wentworth's records about paying your Rangers."

Iain knew Haviland was lying.

But why?

Iain fought to keep his temper in check. "The officers who served under him can attest that I speak the truth."

"Most of his officers were slain, as I'm sure you know." Haviland flicked a lacy wrist, glanced at his well-shaped nails. "Some are no doubt still in New York at Fort Edward. Others are on their way back to London."

"The men who fought as Rangers — they are good men, men with wives and bairns, men who risked their lives for five long years, sufferin' deprivations you cannae imagine. And now, after the Rangers helped Britain win this victory, you prepare for your Christmas feastin' and deny them their due?"

"The Rangers are known for hitting marks. If they are hungry, let them hunt," Haviland answered, his tone of voice disdainful. "You made it clear more than once that you and your men fought not for the Crown, but for your fellow colonists. I suggest you turn to them if you wish to be paid. If Governor Colden and his council appreciate your services, perhaps they can find the coin."

Connor started forward. "You bloody — "

"*Uist!*" Iain silenced Connor, held out his arm to stop him. "This arrangement stood through five long years of war. Would you dishonor the reputation of the British Army by breakin' it now?"

All pretext of politeness disappeared, Haviland's loathing and resentment clear to see. "The British Army had no need for men such as you. Why Wentworth favored you, I know not, but I will not reward your insolence."

Iain thought carefully about his next words. He could not fail the men, and yet he felt certain that Haviland would not hesitate to throw him and his brothers in the guardhouse if they spoke carelessly. "What if I bring you proof that Wentworth paid the Rangers?"

"If proof exists, I shall be glad to see it, and I should gladly honor the Crown's obligation."

"Then I shall return tomorrow wi' proof to satisfy you." He motioned to his brothers. "Come."

He walked down the hallway, his brothers close behind him. Without speaking, they took back their weapons from the lieutenant, who was struggling to set them down without dropping them or cutting himself. Then they stepped outside, cold air hitting Iain full on the face, helping to clear the fog of rage from his mind.

"He's lyin'!" Connor hissed.

"Aye, he's lyin'," Morgan agreed. "But how are we to prove that? Do you think the paymaster will take our word over that bastard Haviland's?"

"There's but one way to prove what is owed to the men." Iain started toward the fort's gates. "We must find Wentworth."

Lord William Wentworth sat beneath thick blankets on a chair before the hearth, trying to doze, his feet propped up on a footstool. Laudanum had left a bitter taste on his tongue, his mouth dry, but at least the pain had diminished. He shivered, drew the blankets tighter about himself, feeling chilled to the bone despite the blazing fire.

His physicians had been right. The long journey from Fort Ticonderoga to Fort Edward and then on to Albany had brought back his fever and, with it, the terrible pain where his wounds had festered.

His eyes drifted shut, oblivion slowly taking him, strains of harpsichord music drifting through his dreams. 'Twas a Christmas carol.

He remembered now. Sarah had been playing upon the harpsichord he'd given her, the sweet music filling him with—

A knock woke him.

"My lord, it is I, Cooke. I must speak with you on an urgent matter."

William shivered beneath his blanket, bit back a curse. "Come in."

Behind him, the door opened and closed, letting in a rush of cold air.

Cooke appeared at his side, gave a bow. "My lord, I — "

"Yes, get to it, man!" William ached with weariness.

Cooke frowned. "Your fever has returned. I shall fetch Doctor—"

"No! No." William was tired of doctors and their pitying glances. "I've been bled enough. I wish only to sleep. What is it you've come to tell me? Speak, and be gone."

"The MacKinnon brothers are in Albany, my lord, and they are looking for you."

William had left the letter and the cracked black king as a way of saying farewell to Lady Anne and to Sarah. He should have thought that would be obvious to them. But the three brothers had tried to follow him that night, calling for him, riding after him in the snow, forcing him and Cooke to drive their mounts hard. Cooke had urged William to stop, to stay the night at the MacKinnon farm, but he had refused.

William did not wish to be seen like this — not by the MacKinnon brothers, not by his niece, not by anyone. That's why he'd kept to these rooms since arriving in Albany and why Cooke was his only contact with the world beyond these walls.

"Go on."

"I spied them entering The Fife and Drum, the pub frequented by our officers down on the— "

"I am familiar with Albany, Captain."

"I entered behind them, kept to the shadows, and overheard them asking if anyone had seen you. They said that it was essential for them to find you as they needed to speak with you on a matter of great urgency and— "

"They are simply trying to find me, trying to flush me out for Sarah's sake so that they can bring me back and see what's become of me. I do not wish to be seen by them, Captain. Do you understand? Are you quite certain they didn't notice you? For if they did, they'll simply follow you and..." Some part of William realized that his words were little more than fevered raving. "I need water."

He hated being this weak, helpless like a child.

Captain Cooke immediately poured water for him from a porcelain pitcher and held out a glass. "You should not be alone, my lord."

William drank, the water soothing his parched throat, then set the glass aside. "Did they reveal the nature of this urgent matter? Is my niece...?"

She'd been well and alive a few nights back. She'd recognized the chess piece he'd left on MacKinnon's doorstep and had run from the house, barefoot and clad only in her shift, crying out for him — proof that she did not hate him despite everything he'd done to keep her and Connor MacKinnon apart.

What if running barefoot in the snow had left her ill?

"I am certain she is well, my lord." Cooke handed him another cup of water. "Knowing you would wish to know their business, I made some inquiries. It seems they have a dispute with Haviland, my lord, and need your help."

CHAPTER FIVE

Amalie reached out and tied the string she'd bound to the end of the pine garland to the nail Joseph had driven into the wall, hoping it would be strong enough to hold the garland in place. "What do you think?"

Joseph reached up, caught her about the waist, and lowered her to the floor from the chair she'd been standing on, a grin tugging at his lips. "I think it is strange to hang branches from trees inside your home when there is a forest outside your door. If you wish to see trees, why not go outside?"

Amalie couldn't help but smile. "It is a way of celebrating the season. And the scent of pine — is it not sweet?"

She sniffed the air, loving the freshness.

He grinned. "You can smell pine even better if you go into the forest."

"It is far too cold to spend our days out of doors."

Joseph chuckled, putting the chair back in its place at the table.

She turned slowly, taking in the sight of the sitting room, only the discord between her and Morgan marring the moment. *"Bien!"*

She, Annie, and Sarah had thrown themselves into preparing for Christmas, first decorating Iain and Annie's house and then Morgan and Amalie's. This Christmas would be a happy one, even if their men should find themselves unable to return from Albany in time. The three of them had discussed it at length and had decided that from now on Christmas at the MacKinnon farm would blend together all of their traditions — Catholic and Protestant, Scottish, English, and French.

Pine garlands hung around the doors and windows and above the hearth as had been the custom for Annie's and Sarah's families. Advent candles sat in the center of each family's table, surrounded by wreaths of holly that Sarah had made. Slender tapers of precious beeswax sat in brass holders in the windowsills as they had at the abbey when Amalie was a child.

On Christmas Eve, they would light those candles as a sign of welcome to weary travelers, and they would leave a meal on the table of each cabin. There would be no Mass on Christmas Day, for there was no church or priest, but they would pray together and then feast — roasted turkey and venison with gravy, potatoes, corn bread, and pickled vegetables, with Annie's shortbread, sugared plums, and apple pies for dessert.

This blending of traditions might not have entirely pleased the *mère supérieure*, but it brought them all together like the family they had become, starting new traditions that they would pass to their children.

At that thought, Amalie glanced toward the bedroom, where the twins, Lachlan and Connor Joseph, slept, and found herself smiling. Her sons would grow up with something she'd never had — a family, a sense of home.

A thud came from upstairs, followed by Annie and Sarah's muffled laughter — and a groan from Killy, who had been helping them hang pine garlands.

Joseph called up to them. "Are you all right, old woman?"

"Killy is well," Annie answered, clearly fighting not to laugh. "He stood too near the edge and…fell off the chair."

"I'd best help him before he breaks his neck." A grin on his face, Joseph started up the stairs.

From outside came a man's voice. "Hallo in the house!"

This was followed by a low bellowing noise.

In a little more than a heartbeat, Killy and Joseph stood together by the front door, muskets in hand.

Joseph looked out the window, his brow bending in a surprised frown. "I see a man with a wagon."

Amalie peeked outside. A man stood holding the reins of two enormous black draft horses, their traces tied to a farm wagon. "It is Farmer Fairley."

"Oh!"

Amalie turned to find Sarah standing beside Annie at the bottom of the stairs, a shocked expression on her face. Her newborn in her arms, she glanced from Amalie to Annie, then looked over at Joseph and Killy. "Farmer Fairley was supposed to deliver my Christmas gifts to the family, but not until the morning of Christmas Eve."

"It seems Christmas has come early." Killy leaned his musket agains the wall, opened the door, and strode outside, his words drifting back to them. "A good day to you! Killy's the name. What is it you…"

A great bellowing arose, drowning out Killy's voice.

"What kind of gift is that, little sister?" Joseph asked Sarah, a grin on his face as he followed Killy outside.

Sarah glanced at Amalie and Annie, as if to explain. "I thought Connor and his brothers would be home when Farmer Fairley arrived."

Folding her shawl around her baby, she brushed past Amalie and out the door, Amalie and Annie hurrying behind her.

And Amalie saw.

A great bull stood tied to the back of the wagon. Unhappy about its plight, the animal huffed and growled, its head tossing from side to side, great horns slashing the air.

"Mercy!" Annie said beside her.

"Master Fairley, I wasn't expecting you so soon," Sarah said.

"There's a storm headed this way, and my good wife would be most displeased if I should be snowed in here with you and miss her Christmas cookin'." He removed his hat, scratched his head. "Truth be told, I can't be keepin' this bull any longer. The beast has already destroyed one trough and all but brought down my spare cowshed. He's a cantankerous animal."

As if to prove Farmer Fairley's words, the bull chose that moment to crash its head into the back of the wagon, causing the wagon to rock forward and frightening the horses, which whinnied and stamped uneasily at the snowy ground.

Farmer Fairley calmed the horses, holding fast to the reins. "I need your good man to take the beast off my hands."

"My husband is not here, nor are his brothers," Sarah told Farmer Fairley. "They were called away to Albany on a matter of great importance."

Farmer Fairley's eyes narrowed. "You didn't tell them you'd bought the animal, did you? You meant to *surprise* them?"

At the expression on Sarah's face, Farmer Fairley broke into guffaws. "One must take great care with a bull. If it were to get out, it could kill someone or get into another farmer's field and cause havoc."

Sarah's gaze fell to the ground. "I...I didn't know."

Farmer Fairley patted one of his horses on its flank. "You'd best be decidin' what to do with it, for I'll not be takin' that beast back home with me. Show me where you want it, and I'll lead it there for you."

Sarah looked from Killy to Joseph, and Amalie could tell by the expressions on their faces that they hadn't the first idea what to do with an angry bull. Neither of them were farmers. But that wouldn't stop them from taking charge.

Killy pushed up his sleeves. "We'll put him in the dryin' shed, tie him down tight, and see to it he's got food and water. When the boys get home, they'll know what to do with him."

Amalie knew little of farming or animal husbandry, but she had watched many a time while Sister Marie Louise had tended the convent's small herd of cattle, leading the bull from pen to paddock so that it could breed the cows. It had never seemed a challenge, the big animal following wherever Sister Marie Louise led.

Amalie walked around the wagon to get a closer look, amazed at the size of this bull, its coat red and shaggy, its body thick and muscled, its horns long. A rope ran from the ring in its nose to an iron ring fixed to the wagon's frame. She had no doubt that should that rope break, the beast would stampede, raging at all of them.

It eyed her, its pupils dark, the whites of its eyes flashing as she drew nearer.

"Oh, the poor beast!" Amalie drew closer still. "It is frightened."

Sister Marie Louise had never tied a bull in a shed by itself. She'd always made certain the animal had the company of a cow or two to keep it content.

She turned to Annie. "Go and get Nessa from the barn and loose her in the paddock. Spread hay for her and fill the trough with water."

The water would freeze during the night, but it was the best they could do until other arrangements could be made.

Annie nodded and dashed off toward the barn.

Joseph frowned. "What do you know of bulls?"

"I watched one of the sisters tend our herd of cattle at the abbey. I often walked beside her as she led the bull to pasture."

Joseph shook his head. "This beast is mean-spirited. It would be hard for a grown man to tame him, let alone a small woman."

The bull bellowed again, swung its head from side to side, pawed at the snow.

"It has nothing to do with size. It is about mastery," Amalie said, remembering what Sister Marie Louise had once said to another nun who was afraid to go near the bull. She turned to Farmer Fairley. "When the cow has been moved, you can take him and place him with her."

Farmer Fairley nodded. "The company of a good cow ought to calm him. 'Tis more often than not the cows that train the bull."

Killy chuckled and opened his mouth as if to speak, then seemed to think the better of it, his mouth snapping shut.

Farmer Fairley motioned to the back of the wagon. "Why don't you two men unload the rest of it while we're waitin'?"

Amalie looked over at Sarah again, amazed. There was more?

Killy and Joseph walked to the side of the wagon and, together, drew back a heavy sheet of canvas, a wide grin spreading across Killy's face. "A plow — and a fine one at that — and a scythe, too."

Amalie stared over at Sarah, astonished.

Sarah looked as if she feared she'd done something wrong, her gaze drawn repeatedly to the bull, which lowed and huffed. "These are my

Christmas gifts to all of you. I wanted to help in some way, to use my coin to make life on the farm easier."

"Such gifts, Sarah!" Amalie couldn't imagine how much the bull must have cost, much less the plow and scythe. She knew Sarah had been left with a small fortune, but hadn't imagined Sarah would spend so much of it on the farm. "You are very generous."

"You are my family now."

Sarah's simple reply put a lump in Amalie's throat. She understood only too well how it felt to be alone in the world. Until she'd come to live at the farm with Morgan, she'd never had a place she could truly call home. "Yes, we are your family."

"Well, the boys will be surprised when they get back, won't they?" Killy laughed, lifting the scythe out of the wagon and walking over to lean it up against Iain and Annie's cabin.

"That much is certain." Grinning, Joseph hopped into the wagon and lifted up the heavy plow. "I am glad I will be here to see their faces."

The bull bellowed again, lowered its head, and crashed once more against the back of the wagon, making Sarah gasp and nearly knocking Joseph off balance as he tried to lower the plow to Killy.

"I've got it." Killy rested the heavy implement on the ground, chuckling. "Aye, this will be a Christmas to remember."

Amalie saw that Nessa was now in the paddock, Annie spreading hay on the snow-packed ground.

Farmer Fairley saw, too. He handed the horse's reins to Killy, then got something out of the back of the wagon — a thick rod.

Another bellow, another crash.

"Quit your caterwaulin'!" Farmer Fairley walked to the back of the wagon, hit the bull with a stick to make it step back, and unbound the rope, glancing over at Amalie. "You'd best move aside, mistress. Bulls are troublesome. You can never tell when — "

The bull bellowed and turned as if to run, the sudden motion causing Farmer Fairley to drop the rod. For a moment, Amalie feared the bull would charge the poor farmer, perhaps even gore him.

Without thinking, she stepped between the farmer and the terrified animal, raised her hand, and struck the bull as hard as she could on its nose. "*Non!*"

It quietened at once, turning its head to gaze at her.

Any fear she'd felt subsided. She took the rope from a startled Farmer Fairley, then chastised the bull in her native tongue. "*Comporte-toi bien ou tu seras castré et finiras dans ma marmite!*"

Behave, or you will be gelded and put in my stewpot!

The animal followed docilely as she led it toward the paddock.

From behind her she heard Joseph let out a breath.

And then Killy spoke. "I'll be damned."

Connor and his brothers began their second full day in Albany by heading below stairs to break their fast and talk over their plans, careful to speak only in Gaelic lest they be overheard and their words carried to Haviland.

"Either Wentworth has already set sail for New York, or he doesna wish to be found," Iain said.

Connor nodded his agreement, finishing his breakfast of eggs, sausages, and bread with a swallow of hot coffee. "What are you goin' to say to Haviland? We've no more proof today than we did yesterday."

"I dinnae ken just yet." Iain looked across the rough-hewn table at Connor. "But we owe it to the men no' to give up."

Morgan tore off another bite of bread. "If it weren't so near Christmas, I'd say we should journey to Fort Edward and seek witnesses there."

"What we need are the army ledgers Wentworth's clerk kept."

Connor thought he knew where those ledgers were. "Haviland probably has them and knows full well he's cheatin' the Rangers. He's lyin' to us, the *mac an uilc.*"

Son of evil.

"Wentworth is gone, and so Haviland sees his chance to bring the Rangers low." Morgan tossed back the last of his coffee. "I wonder if he kept their pay for himself."

Iain's face settled into a scowl. "I wouldna put such a thing past him, but we cannae accuse him wi'out proof."

Anger churned in Connor's gut to think that any man could so blithely deprive another of what was rightly his. "I've a mind to take what belongs to the men from the next British supply train."

Iain arched a dark brow. "We've only just freed the MacKinnon name from the taint of murder."

"Now you would see us hanged for thieves?" Morgan chuckled.

Connor shrugged. "At least we'd be guilty."

It enraged him to think of men who'd served so faithfully — some of them, like Killy, McHugh, and Forbes, from the earliest days of the war — being deprived of the coin they'd earned by risking their lives. He had no doubt they and their families would make it through the winter. A canny man could provide for his family by harvesting the bounty of the forest, and the Rangers were cannier than most. But after all they'd endured, they shouldn't have to face such deprivation.

Haviland, pampered officer that he was, would never understand the hardship the Rangers had faced. Long marches in sweltrie heat and bitter cold. Gnawing hunger. Exhaustion. And always death — death that stalked them from behind every hillock and tree, death that cut down their comrades beside them, death that turned wives to widows and left the bodies of heroes to molder on the forest floor.

Nay, Haviland could not understand. Yet, how could he deny the service the Rangers had rendered? These men had fought for Britain, turning the tide of the war, bringing victory when British generals had known only defeat.

"We will go to Haviland and demand to see Wentworth's ledgers. All the proof we need is there."

"And if he refuses to produce them?" Morgan asked.

"We'll pay the men ourselves," Iain said. "I'll ask Annie to sell some of her mother's jewels to see the men well settled. I'm certain she'll agree."

Connor and Morgan exchanged a glance. Although the wealth a woman brought to her marriage belonged by law to her husband, Iain had intended never to touch Annie's jewels, her inheritance from her mother. "Nay, I'll ask Sarah to part wi' some of the coin Wentworth left for her. Those jewels are all Annie has of her family."

Their discussion was interrupted when Miss Janssen appeared at their table. She'd watched them all morning, seeming pensive now rather than angry.

"Pardon me." She looked over at Connor. "May I speak with you?"

Connor stood and followed her a short distance.

"Is what you've told me true? Does Killy truly feel...affection for me?"

Connor forgot his rage for a moment. "Aye, miss, he does. I heard him say wi' my own ears that he was afraid to ask you to wed him for fear you'd refuse."

She held Connor's gaze for a good, long moment, as if measuring the truth of his words, then gave a nod as if something had been decided, her lips curving into the first smile he'd ever seen on her face. "I'll bring you all more coffee."

And Connor saw why Killy thought her handsome. Without a frown weighing down her features, she was quite bonnie.

They paid for their room and board and left the tavern, making their way up the hill toward the fort, snow falling in thick, fat flakes.

Connor looked up at the leaden sky. "It will be a long trek home."

"Aye." Morgan trudged along on his left. "We must leave soon if we wish to make it back to the farm in time for Christmas Eve."

Connor felt that pull — the tug of home and hearth, wife and child. He, too, wished to be home for Christmas. He wanted to see Sarah's eyes when he slipped that gold wedding band on her finger, wanted to watch it glint in the candlelight as she played at her harpsichord, wanted to hold his son and kiss his sweet, downy hair.

But their duty to the men came first. It would not do for them to enjoy the warmth of their fires and the company of their women when men who'd fought for them suffered want. That would be the same as turning their backs on their clan. For the Rangers *were* their clan, bound to them as brothers by the blood they'd lost and spilled together.

Iain's voice interrupted Connor's thoughts. "Do naugh' that might cause Haviland to arrest us. Dinnae threaten him. Dinnae speak a word that he might deem treasonous."

Connor realized that Iain was looking at him. "Why do you speak only to me and no' to Morgan?"

"Because I ken my brothers well." A grin tugged at Iain's lips.

They reached the fort quickly and were immediately given an audience with Haviland. This unnerved Connor, a shadow of warning passing over his heart. He glanced about covertly, and what he saw was not to his liking.

"Aye, I see it," Morgan said in Gaelic. "There are twice the number of redcoats at the door, and Haviland has posted sentries in the hallway that were not there yesterday."

"He must be expectin' trouble," Iain said.

"Or hopin' for it." Connor's sense of foreboding grew stronger. "They haven't tried to disarm us this time."

Something about it reminded him of the day so long ago when Wentworth had arrested them on false charges of murder. But Haviland was not Wentworth, for he wasn't nearly as wily, nor did his cruelty serve a purpose. Wentworth had wanted to force them to fight for him. Haviland seemed to seek only to humiliate them — or ruin them.

They found Haviland at Wentworth's writing table just as he'd been yesterday. "You have returned, MacKinnon. Show me proof."

Iain stepped forward. "We searched the city, but couldna find a single officer or soldier who'd served wi' Wentworth, so I have nothin' more to show you than I did yesterday. But I swear to you that Wentworth saw to the payin' of my men. The proof you seek is written in the ledgers his clerk kept at Fort Edward. Either those ledgers are already here in your possession, or they remain at Fort Edward. If you would bring them, this matter could be easily settled."

"Wentworth's ledgers? I know not what became of them. I passed through Fort Edward on my way here, of course, but I saw no ledgers. Perhaps they were lost in the same battle where he was taken captive. Although I could dispatch a messenger and ask the commanding officer at Edward to search for them, there are so few troops remaining at my disposal that I would consider that a waste of His Majesty's resources. Without proof, MacKinnon, I cannot and will not pay your Rangers."

Haviland spoke the last word with contempt, his lip curling.

Neach dìolain! Bastard!

Connor bit his tongue, recalling Iain's admonition not to say anything that might get them arrested.

"These *Rangers* turned the tide of the war. By their blood, British troops were kept safe on the march. Through their skill wi' shootin' marks, trackin' and woodcraft, the Crown won many victories. And now you would break Britain's word to them, deprivin' them of their wages and leavin' their families to go hungry at Christmastide?"

"I don't know of any promises made to the Rangers, MacKinnon," Haviland replied in a silky voice, rising to his feet. "As for their much-vaunted woodcraft, their ability to skulk through the forest like heathen Indians *does* lend itself to performing certain tasks, but that hardly makes the Rangers soldiers. You and your men are nothing more than the raffish spawn of exiles."

Connor felt his teeth grind, his fists clenching as he fought to keep them at his side and not slam the whoreson in the face.

But Haviland went on. "When I look at you, MacKinnon, do you know what I see? I see the sons of a Jacobite traitor. One of your brothers was convicted of treason and only stands here today because he managed somehow to escape the hangman."

Iain cut Haviland off, his voice booming through the small room. "Morgan was never a traitor! Governor DeLancy himself pardoned— "

"And your younger brother — I've heard the rumors. I know that he seduced Wentworth's niece and got her with child. Perhaps *he* arranged the attack that led to her death. Perhaps he— "

"*Neach dìolain*!" Connor lunged toward Haviland, only to come up short when he saw that Iain had already grabbed the bastard by the throat.

"Dinnae you be talkin' about my brothers or poor Lady Sarah like that, Haviland, you filthy son of a whore!"

Haviland jerked away, a mix of fear and excitement on his face, calling to the sentries Connor had forgotten in his fury. "Arrest these men!"

In a heartbeat, redcoats filled the room, and Connor found himself and his brothers held at bayonet point as Haviland watched, gloating.

"Put them in irons. Take them to the guardhouse."

"Belay that order, and stand down!"

Connor's head jerked around toward the sound of the familiar voice. And there in the doorway in full uniform, he stood. "*Wentworth!*"

CHAPTER SIX

William saw the astonishment on the faces of the three MacKinnon brothers — and the shock they quickly hid at the sight of him. He saw a different kind of surprise on Haviland's face and something else, too — fear.

He addressed the Regulars. "Stand down, I said! You are dismissed."

The Regulars hesitated for a moment, looking to Haviland, who spluttered, "Y-you are not in command here."

William turned to Cooke. "Has Haviland's promotion been confirmed, Captain?"

"Aye, my lord, but even so, you are still the senior officer."

William turned back to Haviland. "I outrank you — in every way."

Satisfied, the Regulars hurried out of the room, most of them averting their gazes as they passed William, clearly trying not to look at him. He couldn't blame them.

Even with a wig, his appearance was monstrous.

"Son of a whore." William strode toward Haviland, repeating what Iain MacKinnon had just called him. "Was your mother a whore, Haviland? I know nothing about her."

"My mother was a chaste and respectable woman." Haviland glared at him.

William glanced about the office that had once been his. His gaze fell upon the bookshelves to his left. "My mother is a royal princess, the daughter of our recently departed sovereign and aunt to His Majesty King George III."

Haviland hated being reminded of William's royal bloodline, but William wasn't bringing this up merely to irritate the man.

"I am aware of your lineage, my lord."

"Indeed." William turned and fixed Haviland with a hard gaze. "Why, then, do you dishonor me by breaking the promises I made to the MacKinnon brothers and their men on the Crown's behalf? Word is all over Albany that MacKinnon's Rangers have been denied their wages by the Crown."

Haviland opened his mouth, but nothing came out.

Fighting a wave of dizziness, William pointed to five familiar tomes on the bookshelf. "Aren't those my ledgers? Cooke, would you please examine them?"

"Certainly, my lord." Cooke retrieved the volumes, flipped through them, then held them out for William to see. "These are, indeed, your ledgers from Fort Edward."

Wentworth glanced down at his clerk's familiar writing on the page. "You know full well that the Crown was obligated to pay the Rangers, Haviland, and yet you lied to MacKinnon. You dishonor the king and country you claim to serve — a reckless action for a man with your *lofty* ambitions."

Haviland gave a perfunctory bow, but there was loathing in his eyes. "I regret my actions, my lord. I simply do not understand what you see in these rough men."

"Your lack of vision where the Rangers are concerned is of little import to me. Your lack of character is. You will apologize to these men. Now."

William might have found the horror on Haviland's face amusing had he not been so very ill and in so much pain.

Haviland spoke the words, but refused to look at the brothers. "My apologies."

"Captain Cooke, please take the Brigadier General into the next room and help him and his clerk determine the exact amount that is owed to each Ranger. See to it that the wages are counted out within the hour, and make some provision to see their pay delivered before Christmas Eve."

"Yes, my lord."

"Now leave us. Close the door behind you, and see that we are not disturbed."

"I am your most humble servant, my lord." Cooke gave a smart bow, then turned toward the door, motioning for Haviland to follow. "This way, sir."

Hatred blazing in his eyes, Haviland gave William a stiff bow and turned to go.

"One last thing, Haviland." William glared at him, at last letting his rage show. "If I hear that you have dishonored the memory of my dear belated niece again, if you even mention her name or repeat what you said today, *I will not rest* until I have had satisfaction. Do you understand?"

"Y-yes, my lord. My apologies."

"Get out of my sight!" William waited until Cooke had closed the door behind him, then made his way with careful steps to the chair on the other side of his writing table and sat, his legs barely able to hold his weight.

Iain MacKinnon spoke first. "You are unwell."

"Does it please the three of you to see me thus? Do you revel to see that bastard Wentworth at last brought down?" He had not wanted them to see him in this condition — weak, scarred, in pain.

The three brothers frowned, shaking their heads in protest.

"I wouldna wish such sufferin' on my worst enemy," Connor answered.

"Nor would I," Morgan answered.

Iain glared at him. "You misjudge us."

Perhaps Iain was right. Perhaps William had misjudged them all along.

He fought to keep his teeth from chattering. "How is Lady Anne?"

"My wife fares well, as do our children. She sends her regards."

Ah, sweet Lady Anne! How William would love to see her one last time. He had tried every means he could devise to win her to his bed, even asking her to be his mistress, but she had chosen Iain MacKinnon, a man without wealth or titles.

William turned his gaze to Connor and asked the question that had troubled him most these long months. "How is Sarah?"

"She is well. She gave birth to our son two weeks past. She named him William."

William already knew this, of course, but to hear it directly from Connor put his mind at ease. He found himself smiling. "How awkward that must have been for you to have a son named after me."

Not that it wasn't also awkward for William. Connor MacKinnon, youngest son of an exiled Jacobite laird, was now William's nephew by marriage, his barbarian Highland blood mingled with Sarah's. No one in England would ever know this, of course, as everyone believed that Sarah had been killed last summer.

Then Connor drew something out of his coat, stepped forward, and held it out for William. "She bade me give you this."

A letter.

William took it, stared down at his name spelled out in Sarah's delicate handwriting, and was overtaken by an unexpected rush of emotion. Unwilling to open it in front of anyone, he tucked it inside his waistcoat.

"She was sore fashed that you rode away and didna stop to see her."

"Does she speak well of me?" William had to know.

"Aye, my lord. She misses you and worries about you."

Had Connor MacKinnon just called him "my lord"?

By God, he had!

This so astonished William that he almost laughed.

Then Iain spoke. "You are welcome in our home. Let us procure a wagon and get you back to the farm where Annie can tend your hurts. She has a deft hand wi' healin'. You'll be strong again in no time."

William shook his head, their pity and this shift in their behavior toward him making him feel vulnerable in a way he'd never felt before. "I do not wish for Lady Anne or Sarah to see me like this."

Oh, how he hated to admit that!

Morgan frowned. "Dinnae be foolish! You fought like a soldier, a true warrior. There is no shame in that. Whatever scars you bear are marks of honor."

"And what of Sarah?" Connor asked. "She loves you. Helpin' to care for you would bring her great joy. Also, she wants very much for you to see our son. If you were to come wi' us and spend Christmas wi' her, she — "

"No!" William spoke the word more sharply than he'd intended, perhaps because Connor's words tempted him sorely or perhaps because, without laudanum, his pain was becoming most difficult to bear. "I said farewell to my niece on the battlefield. I would have her remember me as I was."

Morgan looked from Iain to Connor, then slipped out of his tumpline pack, reached inside, and drew out a small pot. "Spread this salve on your wounds mornin', noon, and night. It burns like hellfire, but it will stop them from festerin'."

"'Twas this potion Annie used upon my back after you had me flogged and on Connor's shoulder when he was shot," Iain said.

The brothers went on at length about the number of men whose lives and limbs the concoction had purportedly saved until William was quite convinced to try it no matter how horribly it stung.

He picked up the little pot. "My thanks."

"And dinnae be lettin' the physicians bleed you," Morgan added. "They dinnae ken what they're about. Willow bark tea is better for a fever than bleedin' a man."

William forced himself to his feet, one hand on the writing table for balance. "Now it is time you went on your way. Cooke will see to it that the accounts are settled and the men paid, though it may take some time to reach all of them now that winter has set in. I regret that Haviland did not discharge his duty as he should have."

"'Twas no' your doin'," Iain said. "Our thanks for comin' to our aid today."

William looked from Iain to Morgan to Connor. During the long months of his captivity, he'd thought more than once about what he'd say to the MacKinnon brothers should he live to see them again. The horrors he'd seen, the pain he'd suffered, had given him a new appreciation for them and for their survival skills — and their endurance.

Still, he would not apologize. Aye, he had used foul means to press them into service, but their skill had helped ensure victory for Britain, winning accolades for William and turning the MacKinnon brothers and their men into legends.

Long after William's name was forgotten on this frontier, men would still tell stories of MacKinnon's Rangers.

He offered Iain his hand, struggling to find the right words. "It was an honor to be your commanding officer. I thank you for your service, however reluctant it might have been. You fought with uncommon valor."

"I cannae forgi' nor forget what you did to me and my brothers, nor the wrongs you've done to Annie, Amalie, and Sarah," Iain said, taking his hand in a firm grasp, "but you are not wi'out honor. Let the enmity between us end here and now."

At those words, the weight on William's shoulders grew lighter.

Morgan held out his hand. "You balanced the scales atween us when you helped me escape the hangman's noose and secured my pardon. For my part, I forgi'e you."

"Of the three of you, I trusted you the most." William shook Morgan's hand, then turned to Connor. "Tell Sarah that I...love her. Take care of her."

"I promise you she will be safe and want for naugh' so long as there is life in my body." Connor clasped his hand, and they shook. "There have been days when I've cursed you. I once vowed to kill you. But many's the time you came unexpectedly to our aid — such as today. It is those times I will remember."

Shivering with fever, William released Connor's hand. "Farewell."

He sank back into his chair, unable to stand any longer.

"May God's blessings go wi' you," Connor said.

The brothers turned as one and walked out the door.

Iain paused in the doorway, looked back at him, and grinned. "Merry Christmas, Your Immensity."

As William watched them disappear down the hallway, he knew he would never see their like again.

CHAPTER SEVEN

Sarah sat by the fire upstairs nursing little William. Down below, Annie and Amalie were busy preparing the Christmas Eve feast, the house filled with delicious scents — roasted turkey, freshly baked bread, cinnamon from pies. They'd spent most of the day cooking and baking, while Killy and Joseph had carried wood, fetched water for them, and tended to the outside chores.

All the gifts were made. The baking was done. Wood was cut and piled high. Christmas was upon them.

But the men were not yet home.

Sarah's gaze was drawn once again to the window. Outside, heavy snow still fell, clouds concealing the late afternoon sunlight. Connor and his brothers would not make it home through this storm. Nor would she want them to try. If they should leave Albany and find themselves benighted in the forest or lose their way...

She looked down at her baby boy's sweet face. His eyes were now closed, his tiny hands curved into little fists beneath his chin as he sucked contentedly.

"Your father will come."

God, please guide the men safely home to us!

Annie had said little about it, but Sarah knew she feared that Haviland had found some reason to detain them. Sarah prayed that was not true. She remembered only too clearly how much Haviland had seemed to hate Connor from the first moment he'd met him. She could not bear to think of him and his brothers spending Christmas in chains in the cold and dark of the garrison's guardhouse.

She stroked little William's cheek, seeing so much of Connor in his face. She rocked him until he'd finished feeding, then carried him to his cradle and covered him with a felt blanket, tucking a warm rabbit fur around him.

How horrified her mother would be to see Sarah covering her son with a fur, but the fur was soft to the skin and much warmer than the damask coverlet and itchy woolen blanket that Sarah had slept beneath as a child.

She bent down, kissed little William's cheek.

From the distance, she heard that same dreadful bellowing, and knew that the bull was raging again. They'd been forced to bring him and Nessa inside the barn to protect them from the cold. But shut away from Nessa in its own stall, the animal had begun to crash its head against the stall gate, the water trough, the walls of the barn itself, defying even Amalie's attempt to calm it.

Sarah hadn't known any animal could be such trouble. What would Connor and his brother say when they got home and found broken planks and a bent water trough? Would they be grateful for the bull, or would they see it as a burden and her as foolish for having purchased it?

She left her sleeping son and rejoined Annie and Amalie downstairs just in time for Joseph to enter.

"That animal will not settle down." There were snowflakes in his dark hair, and his cheeks were red from the cold. He slipped out of his bearskin coat and hung it from one of the pegs by the door. "Let us hope tomorrow is a warm day, or my brothers may return to find themselves without a barn."

There was a glint of humor in his eyes, but Sarah saw nothing funny in this.

He bent down before the hearth and stretched out his hands to warm them, looking up at her, a grin on his face. "Don't worry, little sister. All will be well."

Sarah rejoined Annie and Amalie in the kitchen and resumed peeling potatoes, ignoring the periodic bellowing from the barn. She, Annie, and Amalie talked and laughed as they worked, doing their best to remain of good cheer, while Killy and Joseph spoke together in the next room, played with Iain Cameron, and kept the dogs from getting underfoot.

Outside the window, snow fell harder, daylight fading and, with it, all hope that the men would make it home for Christmas.

Determined to have their husbands with them in spirit if not in body, the women set the table for eight, adding two extra places for Killy and Joseph, then lingered over the meal's last preparations, arranging the Advent candles and holly wreath just so, fussing over the placement of a cup, building up the fire.

Annie wiped her hands on her apron. "'Tis time for supper."

She spoke the words with a smile on her face, but Sarah could see the worry and resignation in her eyes.

Killy and Joseph washed and joined them at the table, each holding one of Amalie's twins, while Amalie lit the Advent candles and the candle that sat on the window sill, its golden light flickering against the silver of the frost-coated panes.

"May all travelers find shelter tonight," she said. "And may God guide our husbands safely home."

She joined the others at the supper table, a loud bellow perceptible over the crackling of the fire and the happy chatter of children. She slid her hand into Sarah's and Joseph's, and they bowed their heads.

It normally fell to Iain, as head of the family, to say grace. With all of the brothers away, Annie took his place. She had just spoken the first words of blessing when Artair and Beatan leaped up from their place by the hearth, tails wagging, and began to bark and scratch at the door.

From outside, they heard it. "Hallo in the house!"

Iain.

Sarah felt a surge of relief as the door opened and Iain entered.

A broad grin on his face, he tossed something to Killy — a coin purse. "There are your wages, old man—minus one schilling six. The matter is settled. The men are gettin' their pay."

Then Iain stepped inside, making way for three others — Connor, Morgan and...

"Hildie?" Killy gaped at the shape that filled the doorway.

Almost as tall as the men, the woman stood there in a great overcoat, her cheeks red from the cold, mittens on her hands, her hems and boots caked with snow.

Killy turned to Iain, who had taken off his tumpline pack and bearskin coat and was hanging it on its peg. "Why in God's name did you drag the poor woman all the way out here in this storm?"

Iain, his jaw dark with many days' growth of beard, chuckled. "She insisted she come wi' us and wouldna hear otherwise."

Morgan drew his tumpline pack over his shoulders, handing it to Amalie, who had hurried forward to help him. "Miss Janssen kept abreast of us the entire way, never flaggin', never once utterin' a complaint."

"You'd be right proud of her, so you would." Connor grinned, his gaze meeting Sarah's as he closed the door and brought down the bar, shutting out the night and cold.

And she could see he was as relieved to be home as she was to have him home. She hurried over to him, began to help him out of his pack and coat.

Killy rounded the table and walked over to Miss Janssen, who pushed the woolen hat from her head, golden hair spilling around her red cheeks. "Why would you do such a daft thing? Are you tryin' to catch your death out in this?"

Miss Janssen brushed the hair from her face. "Is it true what they say — that you want to marry me but are afraid to ask?"

The room fell silent apart from the happy babble of babies.

Killy's face turned a shade of red Sarah had never seen before. He stared up at Miss Janssen through narrowed eyes. "Aye, it is."

Miss Janssen looked surprised. Had she come all this way in hopes that Killy wanted to marry her? What had she planned to do if he'd said no? Would she have turned on her heels and walked all the long way back to Albany alone?

Miss Janssen gave a nod, drew in a breath, seemed to steel herself. "You're not to lie about in idleness, nor will I permit you to drink my profits. The alehouse will still belong to me. As long as you live under my roof, you'll not show me disrespect, nor will you suffer any other man to put his hands on me. If there are children, you'll be a decent father to them for as long as you live."

Killy glared up at her. "Those are your terms?"

She hesitated for a moment, then her chin went up. "*Ja*. What say you?"

A wide grin broke out on Killy's face. "I accept."

"Then we'll be wed in a binding manner on New Year's Eve and remarried in the Dutch church when the snows allow us to return safely to Albany."

"The New Year is a fortuitous time for a weddin'." Killy's grin faded. "But who is watchin' over the alehouse while you're out here?"

"I left Bram, my brother, to run things. I've served ale every day of my life since I was ten years old. If I want to leave for a few days to take a husband, I will."

Killy chuckled, glancing over at Annie. "I told you she was fierce."

Hildie drew something from inside her coat and held it up for Killy to see. It was a sprig of mistletoe.

Killy stared at it for a moment, then chuckled. "You wild woman."

He rose onto his tiptoes, drew her head down, and kissed her hard upon the lips, drawing cheers and laughter — and putting a blush in Hildie's cheeks.

Through a mist of tears, Sarah looked up into Connor's eyes, felt his arm slide around her waist, and saw that he was as happy for Killy as she.

As laughter died there came a terrible bellowing from the barn.

Sarah had forgotten about the bull.

"What on God's earth is that?" Iain asked, picking up the musket he'd just set aside. "It sounds like a… "

"It's a bull, brother." Joseph grinned. "Sarah has some Christmas gifts for you."

Connor and his brothers looked at Sarah, astonishment on their faces.

Another bellow. A crashing sound. Splintering wood.

Sarah looked up at her husband. "Merry Christmas."

Hildie was getting married.

She could scarce believe it, the strangeness of it leaving her almost numb as Killy helped her out of her wet boots, pack, and coat.

He slipped his hand through hers and led her to a chair by the fire, his fingers warm. "You're shakin' like a leaf, Hildie sweet. Rest here while Annie makes you a hot cup of tea. I'll be back inside before you can miss me."

Hildie looked into the eyes of the man she had just agreed to marry and saw genuine concern. "Th-thank you."

She wasn't accustomed to tenderness from men.

Killy and the other men bundled up and headed out to the barn to see the bull, leaving Hildie alone with the MacKinnon brothers' wives. All were beautiful women, much younger than Hildie, feminine and delicate. Compared to them, she was overly tall, ungainly, and big of bone — a pelican among swans.

One with fair hair and green eyes stepped forward and clasped Hildie's hand, a gracious smile on her pretty face. "I'm Annie, Iain's wife. Welcome to our home. I'll get you a pair of warm, dry socks and make you that cup of tea."

"Many thanks."

So this was Annie MacKinnon. Hildie had heard of her. All the news worth knowing made its way to the alehouse in time. It was said that Annie MacKinnon had been born a noble lady but had married Iain MacKinnon for love. Hildie was tempted to ask if this was true, but knew that to do so on so short an acquaintance would be unforgivably rude.

"The walk was long," she said instead.

Of course the walk was long, Hildie! What a foolish thing to say!

"Aye, 'tis a long journey when the sun is shinin'." Annie set the teakettle on the hob. "I dinnae think I'd have made it."

"I am Amalie — Morgan's wife." A dark-haired woman stepped forward, her arms filled with two wriggling babies so alike in age and appearance that they could only be twins. She spoke with a French accent, but her features told Hildie that she was of mixed heritage — perhaps Indian and French. "You must be chilled to the very bone."

Hildie's toes ached, her fingers, too. "*Ja.* It was very cold."

Then Hildie remembered that Morgan MacKinnon had been thrown out of the Rangers for marrying the daughter of a French officer. Her gaze was drawn back to the babies. She'd never spent much time in the company of other women or with children, for that matter, her entire life spent meeting the needs of hungry men.

"These are our twins, Lachlan and Connor Joseph." Amalie set the babies on the floor, where they crawled about and babbled to one another. She took a pair of knitted socks from Annie, knelt down, and replaced Hildie's sodden socks with the dry ones, hanging the wet ones to dry.

Hildie wiggled her tows. "Thank you."

"Would you like some of Annie's shortbread?" The third woman wrapped a warm shawl around Hildie's shoulders, then presented her with a tray of small cakes. "I am Sarah MacKinnon, Connor's wife."

Hildie was surprised at Sarah's refined tone and the crispness of her English. It was not the English spoken by frontiersmen and their families, nor even that of the British officers who'd stayed at the tavern. It was refined, like that of...

Hildie felt her pulse quicken as she remembered what she'd heard this past summer, whispers in corners about Brigadier General Wentworth's niece, whose name was Sarah. Some said Connor MacKinnon had seduced her and gotten her with child not long before she'd been killed by Indians. But one redcoat had insisted that Lady Sarah hadn't been killed at all, swearing he'd seen her at Fort Ticonderoga with Connor MacKinnon after the battle, safe and very much alive. The other soldiers had laughed at him, but now Hildie knew he'd spoken the truth.

She found herself smiling at this happy realization — and at the thought that a high-born British lady was offering *her* something to eat rather than the reverse. "You are all very kind to welcome me into your home on Christmas Eve."

Annie smiled, setting a place for Hildie at the table. "You're to be Killy's bride, and he is as kin to us. That makes you kin, too."

Hildie bit into the little cake, but was so taken aback by Annie's kind words that it took her a moment to notice the taste. It was both buttery and sweet. She might not know anything about babies, but Hildie knew a great deal about food. "This is good! What do you call it?"

"Shortbread," Sarah answered. "Annie makes it. Have another."

Hildie did. "You must teach me the recipe — that is, if you are willing."

"I'd be most happy to share it." Annie gave her a warm smile. "But tell me Hildie, did you truly walk this entire distance through deep snows on Christmas Eve just to see whether Killy wanted to marry you?"

"*Ja.*" Hildie wiggled her toes again, her feet finally starting to warm. "No man has ever said he wanted to marry me before."

And for a moment, Hildie felt utterly exposed, her answer revealing too much about her to women whose beauty and youth left them unable to understand the woes and loneliness of an aging spinster.

But to her surprise, they smiled.

Amalie caught up one of the twins who was crawling too near the hearth. "I think it is very romantic."

"As do I." Sarah held out the tray of shortbread, offering Hildie another. "But what would you have done if he'd said 'no'?"

Hildie was spared having to come up with an answer when there came a hiss, something boiling over onto hot hearthstones. "Supper will be burnt by the time the men return if we don't pull it from the fire. Here, let me help."

She stood, set the shawl carefully aside, and went to work.

CHAPTER EIGHT

"Then the bull knocked the rod from Farmer Fairley's hand, and I feared the beast would gore him. But Amalie stepped forward and struck it between the eyes, so she did. It hushed and followed her to the paddock, docile as a lamb."

Iain laughed along with everyone else, listening to Killy tell the story of Farmer Fairley and his arrival with the bull. Iain's belly was full, their Christmas Eve feast one of the best he could remember, a few crumbs all that remained of Annie's shortbread and the three apple pies.

"I threatened to turn him into a bullock and put him in my stew pot," Amalie said, her cheeks flushed from laughter.

"I am sorry for the trouble it caused you all," Sarah said, regret on her face.

"Dinnae fash yourself, lass." Connor reached over, rested a reassuring hand atop hers. "No one was hurt."

"All has ended well, little sister," Joseph said in a soothing tone, his affection for Sarah clear. "Do not trouble yourself."

"I thank you for your generosity, Sarah," Iain said. "In truth, I've never seen an animal as fine as that one. With the calves he sires and the coin he brings us in stud fees, the farm shall prosper as it never has afore."

Sarah smiled. "I'm glad."

Dandling one of his twins upon his knee, Morgan turned to Connor and suggested they get the old scythe and plow repaired by a smithy so they could finish the planting and harvesting with twice the speed.

And it struck Iain as it never had before. The war was behind them. He and his brothers had, at long last, settled their differences with Wentworth. God willing, only peace lay ahead.

A sense of relief rolled through him, warm and precious.

There'd been a time when he'd despaired of living to see a winter's night such as this one, a time when he'd been certain that he would die in battle with his brothers beside him, the MacKinnon farm abandoned, all trace of their family lost. But now the fighting was done, and his brothers were here with him. They were husbands now and fathers to a new generation of MacKinnons that would grow up on this land, surrounded by plenty and protected by the peace that their fathers had fought so hard to win.

He let his gaze travel around the room. Annie, holding sleepy Mara in her lap. Iain Cameron playing with Artair and Beatan near the hearth. Amalie, laughing and jesting with Killy about the bull, Lachlan in her arms. Sarah, nursing little William, while Connor sat close beside her. Killy trading glances with the wealthy woman who was about to become his bride. Hildie, looking bemused but happy, too. Morgan, with Connor Joseph on his knee.

Joseph leaned closer, speaking for Iain's ears alone. "The Shining Spirit has been good to you, brother."

Sometimes it seemed to Iain that Joseph could read his mind.

"Aye, God has blessed us. There was a time when I'd no' have been able to imagine such a night as tonight. But what of you, brother? When will you take a wife and father children? Is there no Mahican lass who can win your heart?"

Joseph narrowed his eyes. "You sound like my grannies."

Iain laughed, then stood, mug of ale in hand.

The room fell silent.

He lifted his mug. "Here's to the women for a wonderful Christmas Eve feast, to Killy and Hildie on the occasion of their betrothal, to Sarah for her generosity in bestowing such gifts upon her family — and to the memory of those who gave their lives for the peace we enjoy this Christmastide."

Morgan, Connor, Killy and Joseph stood, raised their tankards, and drank.

Iain looked down at his newest sister-by-marriage. "Sarah, 'tis time for some carols. Would you like to play for us?"

Sarah's face lit up as Iain had known it would. "I should be honored."

"*A deste fideles laeti triumphantes/Venite, venite in Bethlehem.*" Amalie did her best to sing along. She willed herself to seem as cheerful as the others as they sang *chants de Noël* — what the others called Christmas carols — in Scottish Gaelic, French, English, and Latin to the accompaniment of Sarah's beautiful harpsichord. Children played at their feet or slept on the thick bearskin rug that stretched out near Iain and Annie's sitting-room hearth.

Amalie was grateful that the men were safely home and happy that they'd made it back in time for Christmas Eve supper. It had been a fun evening, though Amalie's thoughts had never strayed far from the argument she'd had with Morgan before he'd left for Albany.

He'd claimed she did not understand, but she did. He was afraid she would die in childbed, and so he gave her only part of himself. She could not deny that she still found pleasure with him, but that pleasure was incomplete. She missed the feel of his weight upon her, his deep thrusts inside her, the joy of being possessed wholly by him — and possessing him in return.

In truth, it was *he* who did not understand.

Dared she hope that he'd changed his mind on the long journey?

"Venite adoremus/Venite adoremus/Venite adoremus/Dominum."

The song came to an end, and Amalie clapped with the others. The sound roused little Connor Joseph from his sleep. He whimpered, fussed. Amalie went to him, lifted her son into her arms, his twin, Lachlan, still asleep, thumb in his mouth.

"Sleepy lad!" Morgan ran his hand over little Connor's dark hair, his warm smile and the gentleness in his eyes when he met Amalie's gaze a peace offering. He looked so handsome, his dark hair drawn back in a queue, his jaw dark with stubble.

She willed a smile onto her face and sat in the chair that he offered her, fighting not to cry when he kissed her hair, her emotions at an edge. *"Merci."*

They sang a few more carols, then Iain walked to the fireplace and drew from the mantel the heavy, leather-bound family Bible. Apart from Connor's whimpers, the room fell quiet as Iain opened the thick book to a page marked with a red ribbon and began to read, his deep voice seeming to fill the room.

"And it came to pass in those days, that there went out a decree from Caesar Augustus that all the world should be taxed. This taxin' was first made when Cyrenius was governor of Syria. And all went to be taxed, every one into his own city. Joseph also went up from Galilee, out of the city of Nazareth, into Judaea, unto the city of David, which is called Bethlehem, because he was of the house and lineage of David, to be taxed wi' Mary his espoused wife, bein' great wi' child.

"While they were there, the days were accomplished that she should be delivered. And she brought forth her firstborn Son and wrapped Him in swaddlin' clothes and laid Him in a manger because there was no room for them in the inn."

As Iain read about the angels and shepherds, Amalie thought of a young virgin, unmarried and most unexpectedly with child, her betrothed shocked to find her thus, but compelled by a dream and his own compassion to remain true to her. She thought of blameless Mary, great with child, traveling to Bethlehem on a donkey, the pangs of childbirth coming upon her. She thought of a young mother giving birth to her first child in the chill of a stable with only straw for birthing linens.

If Joseph could be a husband to Mary through such hardship and uncertainty, why could Morgan not be a true husband to Amalie?

She felt something wet on her face — tears — and hastily wiped them away.

Connor walked up the stairs to the room he shared with Sarah. He would be glad when their cabin was finished this spring. Not that living under Iain's roof was a hardship, but a man with a wife had a certain need for privacy. Love play was so much more robust and free when one didn't have to worry about being overheard.

He found Sarah combing her long, honey-brown hair, the baby fast asleep in his cradle, soft furs tucked snugly around him. The washtub sat

before the fire, filled with warm water, his shaving soap and razor beside it
— another act of kindness from his wife. "We've got Cathach settled for
the night. He'll no' be breakin' down his stall."

"Is that what you've named him?" Sarah turned to look at Connor, the
brush still sliding through her hair. "What does it mean?"

"It means 'fighter.'"

She laughed at that. "That is fitting. I hope the damage he wrought is
not too difficult to repair."

Connor began to undress. "We'll need a new trough and a few beams
to repair the stall, but dinnae fash yourself. All will soon be set to rights."

He sank into the warm water with a sigh, the heat soothing away the
lingering chill. He washed himself, trying to find a way to tell her about
Wentworth. All they'd told the others was that Haviland had overlooked
the Rangers and that the matter had been resolved. Connor and his brothers
had agreed that Sarah should be the first to hear the news of Wentworth —
and that she should get the news in private, for it was certain to distress
her. Although he was tempted to wait till after the New Year to tell her so
as not to mar these happy days with sadness, he knew she would see a truth
left untold as a lie, and he would do nothing to make her think her trust in
him was misplaced.

Sarah set her brush aside and walked over to him, taking the
washcloth from his hand to wash his back. "Amalie was crying tonight."

"Aye, I saw." He hoped Morgan had noticed, too. "She and Morgan
must find their way through this. There is naugh' we can do for them."

He thought of the mistletoe he'd hung over Morgan and Amalie's bed.
It had worked for Killy and Miss Janssen. He prayed its magic would help
his stubborn fool of a brother make peace with Amalie.

They spoke of little things while Sarah washed his hair and shaved his jaw, her touch soothing, the joys of being bathed by a wife high on Connor's list of reasons he loved being a married man. He waited until he'd dried off and Sarah had drawn back the bed covers to tell her.

"We saw Wentworth."

She sat on the bed, facing Connor, hands clasped tightly in her lap. "How was my uncle?"

Connor told her the story, leaving out only the details of Wentworth's appearance. "Och, you should have seen Haviland's face when Cooke led him out of the room!"

Sarah smiled, but it was a sad smile. "I am glad he was able to come to your aid — and I'm glad Captain Cooke is with him. Did you give him my letter?"

"Aye, I gave him the letter. He didna read it while we were there, but tucked it inside his waistcoat."

"Did…did he tell you why he refused to see me that night?"

Connor sat beside her and took her hands, knowing the moment had come. "Sarah, he didna come inside because he didna wish you to see him."

"What are you telling me?"

He could find no way to blunt the edge of his next words. "They cut off his right ear and then burned the wound, likely to staunch the bleedin'. His face is unscathed, but his neck and the side of his head…"

Sarah's eyes closed, tears streaming from beneath her lashes, her voice an anguished whisper. "*Uncle William!*"

Connor drew her into his arms and held her, offering her what comfort he could. He'd known this would be hard for her. "The wounds had festered, and he was quite sick wi' fever. Morgan gave him a pot of our salve, but he wouldna suffer us to tend him, nor would he make the journey here where Annie could care for him. He said he'd already made his farewells and that he wanted you to remember him as he was. And, Sarah, he asked me to tell you he loves you."

She drew back, looked up at him, surprise on her face, tears staining her cheeks. "Uncle William said that?"

Connor wiped her tears away with his thumbs. "Aye, he did. He also bade me take good care of you, and I swore that I would."

There was more, but Connor waited, letting her take this in.

"He does not blame me?"

Connor feared she still saw it this way, for the war party that had attacked them and captured Wentworth had come for her. Only Wentworth's sacrifice, made at the last moment, had spared Sarah. 'Twas one of the bravest things Connor had seen any man do, let alone a wee English lairdling.

Connor squeezed Sarah's hands, looked into her eyes. "None of that was your doin', Sarah. He doesna blame you, nor will I suffer you to blame yourself. Your uncle made a warrior's choice. He paid the price for your safety willingly, and he bears the scars well. Be *proud* of him, lass."

Connor watched Sarah struggle with her emotions, saw grief give way to something bittersweet.

"I *am* proud of him." She gave Connor a quavering smile. "But I shall miss him."

"As he shall miss you, I'm certain." But there was more. "We made peace wi' him, Sarah. He didna offer his apology, nor did we forgi' him. But we shook hands and agreed to set the past behind us."

Astonishment lit her face — and with it joy. "Oh, Connor! Is this true?"

He chuckled. "Aye, lass."

Then Connor told her all that had been spoken at the end. "Iain turned as we left and said, 'Merry Christmas, Your Immensity.' To tell the truth, I think he liked us callin' him by those names."

There were tears on Sarah's face again, but there was also happiness. "To know there is no longer hatred between you — 'tis the greatest Christmas gift I could imagine."

Connor hoped that wasn't true.

He crossed the room, opened the chest that held his belongings, and drew out the little wooden box that held her wedding band. She needed a bit of solace now, and he much preferred to give this to her in private. "Perhaps this gift will find favor in your heart, too."

Smiling, she took the little box and opened it, her eyes going wide when she saw the gold ring inside. "Oh, Connor!"

"I'm sorry I couldna gi' you a ring when we were wed." There'd been no time. "I hope you'll find this pleasin'."

She lifted it out of the box, held it in her upturned palm. "It is beautiful."

He knew that she'd grown up wearing jewels that would have put this simple ring to shame, but it touched him that she seemed to like it. "There are words engraved inside."

She lifted the ring, tilted it toward the firelight. "I cannot read them. Is that Gaelic? What do they say?"

"*Le mo ghràdh mi agus leum mo ghràdh.* It means 'I am my beloved's, and my beloved is mine.'" He took the ring from her and slid it onto her finger. "I dinnae ken why God saw fit to bring the two of us together. I ken only that I love you and will love you until time itself is at an end. Merry Christmas, princess."

She looked down at the ring, then up at him, cupping his jaw with her palm and smiling through fresh tears. "Merry Christmas."

CHAPTER NINE

Annie settled Miss Janssen on a pallet before the hearth in the sitting room, while Joseph and Killy carried their gear next door to Morgan and Amalie's house, where they would bide the night. Then, exhausted but satisfied, she walked to the bedroom, where she found Iain building up the fire, still naked and damp from his bath.

He looked up when Annie entered. "How is Miss Janssen?"

"She's probably already sleepin'. The poor woman was exhausted."

"I'd never have believed she walked this entire way through deep snows had I not seen it myself. The woman was determined to have a husband, so she was."

"I am happy for her — and Killy, too." Annie began to untie her apron, but Iain's hands took over the task, helping her to undress down to her shift.

"We saw Wentworth," he said.

Annie sat beside him on the bed and listened as he recounted the full story of their days in Albany. When he finished, she swallowed the lump in her throat. "You made peace wi' him?"

Nothing would have surprised her more.

"Aye, we did."

"I hate to think of him feverish and sufferin' alone."

"'Twas of his choosin'. But if I am any judge of Cooke, he'll make certain Wentworth uses the salve."

"I hope so. I wouldna wish for Lord William to perish. For all the wrongs he has done us, there is good inside him."

"Aye," Iain agreed. "But I dinnae wish to be talkin' about Wentworth now."

Iain leaned down, took Annie's mouth in a slow, simmering kiss, one big hand sliding up her thigh, pushing the cloth of her shift out of the way.

Annie's blood began to heat, knowledge of the pleasure Iain could bring her filling her with anticipation. "What do you wish to talk about?"

Iain glanced upward toward the ceiling, his lips curving in a grin.

Annie followed his gaze and saw mistletoe hanging above their bed. What a sweet thing for him to have done! She met his gaze, saw naked desire in his eyes.

He drew her down on the bed beside him. "I dinnae wish to be talkin' at all."

Morgan got Killy and Joseph settled and built up the fires, while Amalie nursed little Lachlan and Connor to sleep and set a meal on the table for the Virgin. He was determined to make peace with his wife tonight, one way or another. He'd seen her tears, had wondered whether it was the tale of the first Christmas that had moved her — or whether her tears were borne of sorrow.

The nagging feeling in his heart told him it was the latter.

Aye, he'd been gone most of a week, but his mind had never wandered far from the troubles that divided them. It stood to reason that their problems had preyed on Amalie's mind as well.

Having laid out the meal, she picked up a brass candleholder in one hand, the flame's light dancing on her beautiful face, her long, dark hair spilling down her back.

Say somethin', you lout!

But before Morgan could find his tongue, she had disappeared into their room.

What could he say? He wouldn't apologize for wanting to protect her. That was his duty as a husband. Why was he expected to watch over her and keep her safe from harm when it came to wild animals and ruthless men, but blamed and condemned when he tried to protect her from the harm that his own seed might cause?

You are selfish and wish only to free yourself from fear.

Her words came back to him, but he brushed them aside. He followed her, closing their bedroom door behind him, not wishing for his words to disturb Killy and Joseph.

She stood there wearing only her nightgown, a woolen shawl around her shoulders, candleholder in her hand.

"I've a gift for you." He drew the velvet bag from his breeches and gave it to her, taking the candleholder to free her hands.

Curiosity on her sweet face, she opened the bag and drew out the combs. "Oh, Morgan! They are lovely!"

He felt a surge of relief, glad that she was pleased with his gift. "They are carved from ivory. When first I saw them, I could not help but imagine them in your hair."

She turned them over in her hand, her enthralled expression giving way to worry. "But how could you afford such a gift?"

"Och, it was well within my means. I would give you the stars if it would prove to you that I love you."

Sadness returned to her face. "I do not doubt your love, Morgan. These are beautiful, but there is no possession I value more than *you* — your body, your heart, your soul — and that is what you refuse to give me. Thank you for the combs. Good night, Morgan. *Joyeux Noël.*"

She turned as if she meant to go sleep in the boys' room again.

Hurt lanced through him, followed by anger.

It was time they settled this.

"Amalie — stop." He went to her.

She stood still, as he'd bidden her, but her gaze was averted.

"'Tis Christmas. You'll be sleepin' in the bed wi' me tonight. I'll no' see you catch your death by sleepin' on the floor."

"As you wish."

Och, Satan's hairy arse! He hadn't meant to speak the words as though they were a command. He didn't want her obedience. He wanted her to be happy.

He set the candleholder down on the bedside table, reached out, cupped her shoulders. "I dinnae wish to see you fall ill."

She said nothing.

"Amalie, for God's sake! How can you blame me when all I want in this world is to keep you and our sons safe?"

She turned to face him. "I do not wish merely to be safe. I want to *live*, Morgan! I want to feel your love, to be your wife in every way!"

"But you *are* my wife in every way."

She shook her head. "You refuse to give me all of yourself, as if I were your mistress or your...your *whore*."

"That's no' the way of it. I cherish you! You bloody well ken that!" He drew a breath, worked to rein in his temper. This was not turning out as he'd hoped. He did not wish to fight with her. "At least tell me why you were weepin'. I saw tears on your face."

Her gaze dropped to the floor. "I was thinking of Mary. An angel came to her and told her she was with child even though she was a virgin, and she never once faltered. Not when Joseph doubted her. Not on the long journey to Bethlehem. Not when she had no choice but to give birth in a stable with only Joseph at her side. It is a story of faith, Morgan. Can you not see? If Joseph found the faith to stand by Mary, why can you not find the faith to stand by me?"

"But I *do* stand by you! I would never forsake you!"

She looked up at him. "In your fear, you already have. By denying me your body, you deny *us*, our marriage, our love. You seek to spare me suffering, but in doing so you deprive me of the joys of being a wife and mother."

And Morgan understood. "You truly want this. You would risk your life for this."

"*Oui*. I want you Morgan — all of you."

He drew her to him, taking her mouth in a slow, deep kiss. She melted against him, returned the kiss with a woman's full passion, her fingers sliding into his hair.

Desire long denied flared to life inside him, and he found himself lifting the soft linen of her nightgown in impatient handfuls, hungry for the feel of her, his cock already hard and straining against the leather of his breeches.

But she was impatient, too, her hands sliding beneath his shirt to caress his chest, then dropping lower, boldly rubbing the bulge of his erection.

There was no time for tenderness or gentle kisses, raw need driving them both.

With a groan, Morgan drew her nightgown over her head, then lifted her off her feet and laid her back on their bed, firelight dancing over her bare breasts, the gentle curve of her belly, the dark curls that hid her sex.

She reached down to fight with the fall of his breeches. "Now, Morgan!"

Hunger pounding though his veins, he pushed her hands aside and drew his cock free, moaning aloud when he pressed the engorged tip against her cleft to find that she was already wet and ready for him.

Her legs wrapped possessively around his waist, drawing him closer as he slid inch by slick inch inside her.

Amalie felt her body arch as Morgan stretched her, filled her, became one with her at last. She bit her lip to keep from crying out, the pleasure astonishing as he began to move, slow strokes quickly building into hard, rapid thrusts that rocked the bedstead. She closed her hands over his forearms, his fingers digging into her hips as he moved faster, thrust harder. Then his thumb found her most sensitive spot, teased it, moving in slick circles over the swollen nub.

She found herself on the crest, bliss drawing tight in her belly, then exploding in a warm rush, a flood of liquid delight. Morgan caught her cries with a kiss, groaning into her mouth as he followed her into oblivion and spilled himself inside her.

He made sweet, slow love to her twice more, once on the bearskin rug before their bedroom fireplace and then again in their bed. It was only as she lay in his arms, about to drift into dreams, that she noticed it.

"*Le gui.*" She did not know what the plant was called in English.

Morgan opened his eyes, a lazy grin spreading on his face when he saw it. "Mistletoe. Where did you find it?"

"I did not put it there." She sat up on one elbow. "I thought you'd hung it."

His brow furrowed. "Nay."

Amalie met Morgan's gaze and knew he was as perplexed as she.

"Hmmm." His eyes narrowed. "My brothers."

Did he believe his brothers had done this?

Amalie blushed to think so.

But then Morgan settled her head against his shoulder, one strong arm holding her close, his other hand stroking her hair. "You know I'd gladly cut out my own heart and throw it in the dirt afore I'd hurt you. Can you forgi'e me, lass?"

"Of course." She slid her hand over his chest, her palm coming to rest over his heartbeat. "But leave your heart where it is, *oui*?"

Christmas Day dawned quietly, snow still falling, the forest around them blanketed in white. Inside the cabins, all were warm and happy. They gathered for a breakfast of salt pork, eggs, and johnny cakes after the animals had been tended, and then exchanged gifts. Everyone received something made by the hands of those who loved them — hats, mittens, shawls, warm nightclothes.

It was clear to Connor, Sarah, Iain and Annie that something had changed overnight between Morgan and Amalie, something that had nothing to do with the beautiful ivory combs in Amalie's dark hair. If their smiling faces hadn't given that away, then their tender touches and stolen glances would have.

But it was Iain who noticed the smug look on his youngest brother's face. "What did you do, for I ken you've done somethin'."

"Do you remember the old oak by the burn?" Connor asked.

"Aye, for certain."

"I cut some mistletoe from its branches and hung it above their bed."

Iain's gaze narrowed. "So that was *you*?"

Connor grinned. "I had plenty, so I nailed some up in your room, too."

"I thought Annie had done that, and I…Well, that's none of your affair. She no doubt thinks *I* hung it, hopin' to seduce her." And Iain remembered. "What of the mistletoe Miss Janssen brought wi' her? Was that your doin', too?"

"I gave her a sprig in Albany and told her it was a gift from Killy."

Iain threw back his head and laughed. "Merry Christmas, brother."

"Merry Christmas." Connor gave him a nudge. "And, Iain, you're welcome."

The week between Christmas and Hogmanay passed in an air of celebration. The men finished the front room and bedroom of Connor and Sarah's cabin, for it was there Killy and Hildie would spend their wedding night. Meanwhile, the women baked pies, cakes, and Black Bun for Hogmanay — what the British called New Year's— and for the wedding. Hildie proved to be quite skilled in the kitchen and stepped in to direct the cooking and baking, but with such humbleness and humor that the other women were most grateful to have her help. And then Hogmanay arrived and, with it, Killy and Hildie's wedding day.

Killy wore his cleanest breeches with a new white shirt, his jaw clean-shaven, his Scotch bonnet washed and repaired.

"I've never seen you so...*clean*," Joseph observed, a grin on his face.

Killy glared at him. "You'd best pretty up your feathers, lad, or you'll never find a bride of your own."

But it was the bride who took everyone's breath away.

Her stature queenly, her blond hair hanging in a thick braid down her back, she wore one of Sarah's old court gowns, a creation of blue silk and pink embroidered roses that Sarah and the other women had altered to fit her, the color a perfect match for the blue of her eyes.

With the MacKinnon brothers, their wives, and Joseph as witnesses, Killy and Hildie stood together before Iain and Annie's hearth, each plighting their troth to the other, their wrists bound together with a strip of MacKinnon plaid. The bride's cheeks were pink, the groom's streaked with tears.

They celebrated with a feast and with music from Sarah's harpsichord, laughter and dancing leaving them all breathless. But the hour grew late, and soon it was time to bid the newlyweds good night.

Killy and Hildie were escorted to the partly completed cabin, which the women had decorated with pine boughs, holly, and ribbons. And then the bride and groom began to argue — loudly.

"You can't mean to carry me!" Hildie said.

"Aye, I do." He glared up at her. "I'd not be able to call myself an Irishman if I let you walk over that threshold."

"You devil! I'm quite capable of walking up those steps and through that door alone. You'll hurt your back and be lame for days. What good will you be to me as a husband then?"

"Hurt my back? Not bloody likely!" Killy glared at Hildie, pushed his sleeves up his arms, and scooped her off her feet, carrying his shrieking bride through the open door of the cabin and leaving his cheering friends to seek their own beds — and pleasures.

And as they turned toward their own cabins, Iain, Morgan, Connor, and Joseph agreed that the New Year would be a good one.

CHAPTER TEN

New Year's Day, 1761

Lord William stood on the deck of the vessel that would carry him to New York Harbor, his gaze fixed on Albany. How different the town now seemed from the day when he'd first arrived. He'd thought it the very edge of civilization then. Yet, its streets were cleaner than those of any English city, its poorest inhabitants better fed and clothed than London's wretched beggars, its leaders educated men.

For almost seven years, it had served as his home.

His gaze dropped to the quay, where men loaded and unloaded cargo, pulled handcarts or drove wagons drawn by draft horses. A trapper, his bundle of furs slung on his back, made his way toward the gates of the stockade to trade. A group of Indians in painted hides huddled together over a campfire, surely also here to trade. Near the gangway below, a sailor bade farewell to a tearful woman and a little boy, their words just beyond William's hearing.

He looked away, his gaze now following the river northward. Up there, beyond stretches of untamed forest at the spot Indians called The Great Carrying Place, stood Fort Edward, watching over the falls of the

Hudson and the route northward. Behind the fort's high walls, William had worked to shape the Crown's strategy, helping to ensure a British victory. How uncertain that victory had seemed in the early days of the war, when the British had lost battle after battle.

Now, the fort held only a thousand Regulars, and Ranger Island — where the MacKinnon brothers and their men had camped with their Mahican allies — was now abandoned, wooden crosses marking the graves of the dead.

"Your quarters are prepared, my lord," Captain Cooke said from behind him. "We should get you below decks and out of this bitter wind. Your fever has only just broken. I wouldn't wish to see it return."

William had no desire to be cooped up in a cabin. "Will you miss Fort Edward, Captain? Will you miss this land?"

Cooke hesitated, perhaps confused by the question.

"Do speak freely."

"Yes, my lord, I shall miss it. When I reach home, I fear I shall struggle to put that which I have seen into words. A forest so thick and vast that it could swallow an army. Mountains that stretch on forever. Lakes as wide as seas. Rivers teeming with fish so that a man can earn his day's catch with his bare hands. And the sky — I've never seen so many stars nor such sunrises and sunsets as I have seen here. Until one has seen such beauty, such violent extremes of nature, with one's own eyes, one simply cannot conceive that such beauty exists."

Conjured by the captain's words, images flashed through William's mind. "You express yourself most eloquently, Captain."

Cooke went on. "And what of the war? Clouds of musket smoke that blot out the sun. A thousand bateaux stretching as far into the distance as the eye can see. War cries echoing through the trees to chill the marrow.

Blood staining the forest floor red. Acts of barbarism and cruelty that defy the most depraved imagination."

Those words conjured up images, too.

"Aye, my lord, I shall miss it — and its people."

William didn't have to ask to know the captain was thinking of the MacKinnon brothers and their Rangers.

"What of you, my lord? Will you miss this place?"

William fought to control his emotions, giving the answer he knew was expected of him. "I suppose I shall, and yet I am most eager to visit my new estates in England and take my place in Lords."

William had come here in hopes of winning a true title and his own lands. He had succeeded. Now it was time to enjoy these hard-earned rewards.

"Quite right you are, my lord."

"What led you to take the king's shilling?" In almost seven years, William had never asked.

"I sought an officer's commission to give some purpose to my youth and to be of service to the Crown. I had also hoped for a bit of adventure."

Those were noble aims. "Did you find what you were seeking?"

"I found far more than I could have imagined, my lord. I think I shall always look back on my days at Fort Edward as the best of my life."

Those words seemed to wrap themselves around an ache that had secreted itself behind William's breastbone.

The best days of his life.

Out of habit, he reached into his coat pocket, his fingers seeking the comfort of the cracked black king. It took a moment to remember that he'd left it at the MacKinnon cabin, a farewell to Lady Anne and Sarah.

He swallowed, fighting a strange tightness in his throat. "Never forget what happened here, Captain."

"I would not be able to forget even should I wish it, my lord."

The young captain's thoughts were most certainly on the battles fought and won, but William's drifted to Sarah and those long, terrible months of captivity. Much to his own surprise, he had done something selfless, buying Sarah's survival and her happiness with his own blood. And she *was* happy.

The letter she'd written to him left no doubt. He'd read it more than a dozen times already, committing it to memory. After expressing her worry for him, Sarah had described at length the happiness of her marriage, the joy she felt at being able to play her harpsichord whenever she felt the desire, the love she felt for her newborn son. She had even praised the life of a farm wife, saying that she felt her days now had a purpose.

"Compared to these happy times, my life in London seems dreary and distant, like an unquiet dream from which I am most grateful to have awoken. I was a bird in a gilded cage, and through your courage and sacrifice, you set me free. I pray that one day I shall be able to express my gratitude to you in person, but if this be my last chance to reach you, then know that I shall forever hold you in my heart."

As he thought about her words, the ache behind William's breastbone began to lessen, for although he would never set foot on these shores again, he was leaving the noblest part of himself behind — with Sarah and her son.

Behind him, the captain made ready to sail, shouting commands to his crew.

"Wouldn't you be more comfortable in your cabin, my lord? The wind is frightfully cold. It would be most distressing if you should fall ill again."

"I feel quite well, I assure you."

The salve the MacKinnon brothers had given him had worked. Though the pain the ointment caused had been all but unendurable, his wounds no longer festered. After months of pain and fever, William was finally beginning to heal.

He felt the ship lurch beneath his feet, the river's current catching the vessel and carrying it away from the quay and downriver. He heard the crack of the sails as they were lowered and caught the wind, the ship picking up speed.

The frigid breeze seemed to blow through him, chilling him to his skin as Albany faded in the distance, but still William kept his watch at the stern, his gaze fixed northward. Then the sun broke free of the forest to the east, its lighting spilling across a landscape of pristine white.

William sucked in a breath, the sight staggering. He looked his fill, drinking in the view, knowing he would never see such untrammeled beauty again.

"Farewell, Sarah."

The wind carried his words away.

ALSO BY PAMELA CLARE

Historical Romance

Kenleigh-Blakewell Family Saga

Sweet Release (Book 1)

Carnal Gift (Book 2)

Ride the Fire (Book 3)

MacKinnon's Rangers

Surrender (Book 1)

Untamed (Book 2)

Defiant (Book 3)

Romantic Suspense

I-Team Series

Extreme Exposure (Book 1)

Heaven Can't Wait (Book 1.5)

Hard Evidence (Book 2)

Unlawful Contact (Book 3)

Naked Edge (Book 4)

Breaking Point (Book 5)

Skin Deep (Book 5.5)

First Strike (Book 5.9)

Striking Distance (Book 6)

ABOUT THE AUTHOR

USA Today best-selling author Pamela Clare began her writing career as a columnist and investigative reporter and eventually became the first woman editor-in-chief of two different newspapers. Along the way, she and her team won numerous state and national honors, including the National Journalism Award for Public Service. In 2011, Clare was awarded the Keeper of the Flame Lifetime Achievement Award. A single mother with two sons, she writes historical romance and contemporary romantic suspense at the foot of Colorado's beautiful Rocky Mountains. To learn more about her or her books, visit her website, www.pamelaclare.com.

You can also keep up with her on Goodreads, on Facebook, on the Rock*It Reads website, or by joining the private Camp Followers group on Facebook. Search for @Pamela_Clare on Twitter to follow her there.

CPSIA information can be obtained at www.ICGtesting.com
Printed in the USA
LVOW10s2353040815

448806LV00005B/394/P